Wilder's Edge

Rebecca–
Go Wild!

WILDER'S EDGE

Diane Bradley

Diane Bradley

– 2014 –

NORTH STAR PRESS OF ST. CLOUD, INC.

Saint Cloud, Minnesota

Published by
North Star Press of St. Cloud, Inc.
P.O. Box 451
St. Cloud, Minnesota 56302

www.nortstarpress.com

www.northstarpress.com

Facebook - North Star Press

Twitter - North Star Press

For Mom
Thank you for writing down my stories when I was young;
not because they were good, but because
you made me believe they were.

One

CRAZY LOON AIR WAS SPEARING clouds over endless lakes and pine trees.

"Sid, I think this gauge is stuck." I gently tapped the dial. The old DHC-2 Beaver was Crazy Loon's entire fleet. Sid was the pilot and owner. From the edge of the co-pilot seat, I watched all the gauges bounce except for one. I tapped harder. I glanced over to see if Sid had noticed, but he hadn't.

Sid was a yakker. Since we had taken off from Minneapolis, it had been two hours of solid chatter and bumpy air. His lucky Vikings hat was crammed onto his head. A graying beard brushed his chest. It was still too cold for his summer shave. He droned on about the fishermen, hunters, and even a dog sled team he had flown up north in the past year. My eyes were glued on the stuck gauge. My fingertip was starting to hurt.

Finally Sid noticed, he leaned over and gave the gauge a sharp rap. "That one always sticks," he claimed. The stuck gauge bounced in time with the others.

I blew out a shaky breath. Sliding back into the seat, my fingers locked firmly around the armrest.

1

"Relax, Henry. In thirty-five years, I've only kinda crashed once," he said with a wink. "Trimmed off some tree tops, knocked off one pontoon. Only counts as half a crash."

"Hah," I forced out. I've known Sid all my life. He'd been flying my folks and me up to Rainy Lake for our summer weekly vacation forever. The prop in front of us whirled in a soft blur as the engine roared. At this height all the lakes look puddle sized, except for Rainy. I packed three weeks ago, before school was even out, begging to come up.

Sid suddenly dropped the right wing down. I took in a tight breath. Sid was a good pilot. I told myself to relax and thought about the summer. This year, I wouldn't be staying for just a week. Glancing over the side window, I saw Rainy below us. I leaned into the window wanting to absorb all of the lake. The granite domed islands and fishing inlets were all waiting for me.

"There's Uncle Mike," I yelled over the hammering of the engine. He stood on the dock of our property, Wilder's Edge. Eighty years ago, my great-grandfather Wilder jumped a freight train in New York that dumped him on the northern Minnesota border. Fur trapping suited him, and he bought this cabin. A Wilder had owned it ever since. Sid dipped the other wing and Uncle Mike began to wave. The whole dock shook as he pumped his arm.

"Let's piss him off." Sid's eyes crinkled with amusement as he swung the plane back across the miles of clear blue water.

"Maybe we shouldn't," I said quietly. Why start the summer on Uncle Mike's bad side?

"Sure we should," he laughed as the plane flew so low to the lake surface that ducks and loons scattered and my uncle stooped. Uncle Mike sent a fist into the air, and Sid yelped a hoot. Circling over the lake, he found open water and bounced the pontoon plane down hard enough to whip my head against the head rest.

Taxiing right up to the dock, Sid reached over to open my door. "You go first. He's got his Border Patrol face on," he chuckled. The door flipped open, and pine air and sun poured in. I stepped out and took in the marshmallow clouds, blue sky, and endless water. I couldn't help but grin.

"Thanks for the ride, Sid," I said, tossing my bag to Uncle Mike. He smiled and caught it. I jumped to the dock.

"Welcome, Henry," Uncle Mike said quickly. Then his smile melted from his face. In his Border Patrol officer voice, he yelled over the idling plane. "Sid, I need to talk to you about that buzzing and scaring the wildlife."

"You weren't scared," Sid laughed louder. "Gotta go. Glad you're here for the summer, Henry," he shouted as the plane pulled away from the dock.

"We'll talk later," Uncle Mike shouted back. His words lost in the roar as the plane accelerated for take-off. My uncle immediately had me in a bear hug. My feet dangled, air squeezed out of me. My face crammed into his flannel shirt that smelled like sun and sweat.

"Glad you're here," he said and then with one hand, he shot-putted me off the dock.

My stomach dropped, my legs cartwheeled and I tried desperately to grab onto something. I couldn't swim a stroke, but Uncle Mike didn't know that. For years I'd been pretending, splashing around on my tiptoes. Uncle Mike's deep rolling laugh followed me as I slammed into the water.

In early June, Rainy Lake was cold enough to steal my breath away. The winter ice had left just weeks before. I felt like an ice cube in lemonade. Water soaked my jeans and sweatshirt. The lake flash froze my skin. I sank. My toes skimmed the rocky bottom. Daylight was far above me. My heart was pounding. Blood rushed through my head as my ears drummed. I fought the urge to breathe, but water seeped into my mouth and I panicked.

Through the depth, I saw Uncle Mike on the dock peering down at me. He was waiting for me to pop up through the surface. I tried to swim. My arms and legs frantically cycled, but nothing happened. I felt more than heard a hard slap as the water brighten. Uncle Mike had jumped in after me. His arm reached down and tugged me up. I was dragged to shore, gasping and coughing. I opened my eyes to see my only cousin, Dylan.

I groaned and it had nothing to do with almost drowning. He was laughing at me. Most days, I loved my cousin or I hated him. Right now he was laughing a little too hard for me to feel like loving him. Uncle Mike sloshed out of the lake right behind me. He picked me up and shook me like a dog. A solid thump on the back forced a weak cough out of me.

"You're okay," Uncle Mike declared more than asked, but peered at me with concern.

I gave another weak cough as water dripped off my nose. "Yeah, I'm good," I gasped.

"Sure?" he asked again. I nodded my head and tried to slow my breathing.

He pushed me towards Dylan. "You guys are good." My uncle smiled and said, "Add learn to swim on that summer fun list, Dylan." A chuckle escaped as he stomped back to the cabin, water squishing in his boots.

It was weird to watch Uncle Mike. He and my dad are identical twins with dark hair and eyes they passed on to Dylan and me. My dad was the same six-foot-six in height, but skinnier. Every time Uncle Mike talked, I expected to hear my dad, but Uncle Mike was louder. I bet he could catch bad guys with one hand and twist their heads off with the other.

Dylan gasped for air between laughing fits. "It wasn't that funny," I said. Pulling back my arm, I gave him a swift thump.

Dylan didn't even feel my punch. "Jeez, Henry, faking it isn't gonna fly this year. Why can't you swim?"

I gave him a long cold stare. "Sure, I can," I said, sarcasm dripping. "Remember, you taught me?" Last summer, teaching me meant dumping the canoe over and over again. I still don't get near the water without a life jacket and Dylan knows that.

He rolled to a stand and brushed the grass from his jeans. I wanted to groan again. He was now more than a head taller than I was, with serious muscles, and he was shaving. I'm two weeks older and don't even have the start of a mustache, no matter what angle of the light.

"What did you do during all those weeks in summer camp?" he asked.

"It wasn't that type of camp," I said, and shivered. This time of year the evenings were still cool. My legs in wet denim weighed a ton as I walked towards the cabin.

Dylan started to laugh again. "You only went to science camp?" he snorted.

"No," I snorted back, "math camp, too." I gave him a hard shove to shut him up, but it only staggered him a bit. It made my elbow ache.

"Well, welcome to Camp Dylan, swimming, fishing, exploring. Repeat often." His return shove sent me flying towards the ground. Eagerly he said, "Get changed. I'll pack the boat."

From the ground, I took in the view. A thin band of smoke from the fireplace drifted up from the chimney. The cabin logs were weathered black and gray and the roof line sagged. It had the basics, basically no Internet, no TV, and no cell phone reception. Despite Dylan, I smiled again, grabbed my bag and with dripping jeans headed for the cabin.

The cabin opened into a small kitchen that flowed into the living room. Yellowed knotty pine covered the cabinets and walls. The uneven wood floors creaked. Worn couches were jammed around a stone fireplace. Large picture windows with sunrise to sunset views of the lake surrounded the space on three sides. Stuffed fish trophies, antique rods and reels, rawhide snowshoes, broken canoe paddles, and deer antlers hung on the walls. Two bedrooms were tucked into the far side along with a set of steps that climbed into the attic.

I lugged my bag upstairs and dumped it at the top. The spare room was the whole upstairs. The exposed roof rafters stopped at a short wall. It was sparse, with a dresser, table, a few chairs, and a couple of beds. I flipped my dripping sweatshirt across the back of the chair and shucked off my wet jeans. I heard Dylan's boat motor sputtering. Unpacking could wait as I threw on dry clothes and headed for the dock.

A lifejacket hit me in the face as I eased into his fourteen-foot boat. "Still alive?" I asked.

Dylan was tinkering with the engine. "Barely," he muttered, adjusting the gas mix to the engine. He loved his boat, but the motor needed constant tweaking and adjusting. The engine finally rattled to a steady drone. He backed the boat away from the dock and headed east.

I buckled my lifejacket and asked, "What's up?"

"We're going fishing."

There were no rods or even a bait bucket, just a sack under Dylan's feet. The motor roared to an ear-screaming pitch. The boat bounced over the waves, snapping my teeth. We're headed into Voyageurs National Park. Our normal fishing spots weren't in that direction.

"Fishing?" I shouted.

"For gold," Dylan yelled over the roar of the motor.

Two

ANYONE WHO HAS PUT A BOAT in on Rainy Lake knows about the gold on Little American Island and Bushyhead and everyone knows that it was mined out over a hundred years ago. So I was really suspicious, "What?" I yelled back. He did the hand to the ear signal and shook his head. He couldn't hear a thing over that monster called his motor. So I sat back to enjoy the ride. I was hoping this was not another Dylan plan. Dylan didn't mean to get me into trouble, but there was that fishing with firecrackers incident and the jumping over the fence to climb the fire tower episode.

Whenever he said, "I've got a really good idea." I swore my stomach cramped. He had a knack for finding adventure and getting caught, but that had never stopped Dylan from trying.

Dylan guided the boat between the red and green buoys that marked a rock free waterway. The sun still felt warm on my back. It was almost seven o'clock. The wind would soon die down, turning the lake glossy smooth. A blue heron flew overhead and golden eye ducks bobbed their butts in the air. They fished for minnows around the buoys. The tangy scent of pine and water flooded the air. I enjoyed sitting in the boat watching the rocky shoreline spotting cabins in among the pines. We pulled into the dock at Little American, and Dylan cut the motor as I jumped out. A landing dock and trail to the mine were maintained by the park. Dylan tossed me the bow rope and I looped it around the dock mooring.

"What are we doing here?" I pulled the boat closer to the dock, roping off the boat's stern.

"Gold hunting." Dylan pulled two sturdy metal pie pans from a bag under his feet. He took a quick look around as he climbed out of the boat. "The coast is clear. We're the only ones here."

"Dylan, the gold is gone." He was making me nervous so I took a look around. "What do you mean the coast is clear?" Ignoring me, he quickly climbed the granite slope towards the mine shaft. I had visited the mine several times over the years. Once one got to the mine, it went almost straight down into the gray bedrock of the island.

At the top of the hill, he stopped for a moment and took another look around, "We're not going to be digging for gold. Henry, do you know how much gold is now?"

Not in the top hundred things I would know. "Nope." I spotted the dark mouth of the mine tunnel through the pine trees.

"It's like a record high. Not hundreds an ounce, a thousand or more," Dylan quickly stated.

I skidded to a stop. "What?"

"Yeah, I know." Dylan added, "Even if we find just flakes of the stuff, it will give us some cash."

I had an allowance for the summer, but nothing to jump up and down about. "So how much is an ounce of gold?"

Dylan pulled a coin out of his pocket. He flipped it and I grabbed it out of the air. It was a quarter. "A little bigger than that, so even if we had a pea size amount of gold, it could be a couple of hundred dollars." Dylan grabbed the quarter back and shoved it into his pocket. "Think of it, Henry. A new boat and motor."

In three more years I would have my driver's permit with the understanding I would have to share Mom's ten-year-old Honda. A black Mustang convertible with chrome wheels just popped into my head. "So if we're not digging, how do we get the gold?" Gold hunting was sounding good.

"You'll see. It'll be stupid easy. Don't know why I didn't think of it before." The mine tunnel appeared, and Dylan entered the tunnel first. He pointed to a thick strip of whitish rock that snaked through the gray granite wall. "This is quartz. Gold is often found near the stuff." He pulled out a flashlight and shined it across the vein.

I studied the quartz and saw nothing that glittered gold. "So what's the game plan here?"

"The gold was all mined out of here years ago, but what if some flakes fell off as they mined the rock and got washed to the bottom of the shaft." He ducked and climbed under the warning barrier and walked down the tunnel. The damp stink of mold and leaf rot hung in the air. He handed me a flashlight. The beam of light bounced around, casting shadows on the walls. Dylan's gotten so big, I could hide in his shadow.

Dylan said in a harsh whisper, "The mine shaft goes in for about a football field. It slopes down, so think of all the water and snow that's been washed down the mine shaft for years and years. There's gotta be gold down there."

I didn't disagree. In fact, this was how all of Dylan's schemes started out. I think they're a great idea and then by the time we're in the middle of them, I'm thinking we're in trouble. My first thought of getting rich quickly faded. This was sounding a bit too easy. My stomach began to ache.

It was getting darker and darker as we went deeper into the tunnel. Moss was sprouting from the damp walls. I shivered and rubbed my arms to ward off the chill. We were climbing straight down when I nearly ran into Dylan. I shined my light around him and saw that the tunnel split in two.

"Call it, Henry. Right or left?"

I always guessed wrong, unless I could calculate the answer. So I was really thinking left tunnel. It was larger, and the rocks looked darker like they had been exposed to the air longer, so I said, "Right."

Dylan plunged down the right tunnel. Moisture caused thick gelatinous goo to grow on the walls. No sunshine reached this far down, and everything looked gray in our flashlight beam. We took about fifty steps down when it came to an abrupt end. "Good choice, Henry," he said in a way that made me want to slug him again.

Dylan waved his flashlight back and forth. He kicked aside dried leaves that hid a thick layer of fist size stones. We picked up some of the rocks and tossed them aside, there was no solid floor. After five minutes of rock tossing, we decided to backtrack and go down the left side.

The left branch wasn't as steep. After five minutes of stepping around rocks, it curved back onto itself to form a small cave. Water was wicking its way down the walls, causing the wet rocks to shine in our light. We both waved our flashlights back and forth across the floor. We hoped for a pool of coarse gravel that would shimmer with gold in our beams. The floor was damp but clear of rocks, stones and gravel.

"There's nothing here." I stooped down and ran my hand across the rock floor. No quartz veins were visible, nothing but the dark gray and black of old granite.

Dylan crouched down beside me and shined the light across the floor to the far wall. "That's weird."

"Yeah," I agreed. "It looks like someone scrubbed the place." There wasn't a speck of loose rock or even a dried leaf.

"It's been sucked dry," Dylan fanned the flashlight beam across the ground. "There're no cracks or opening in the floor so it didn't drain out."

A few large rocks sat along the edge. Dylan gave them a push and they rolled into the middle. We could see where there had been a small pool of water, but there was nothing but a crusty water line and bare rock. Finally I said, "I think someone beat us here," and turned the light back up the tunnel. Goose bumps raced across my skin. I swept the light around the room to make sure no one was there.

"Maybe we should try the Bushyhead gold mine," I suggested. "It was mined the same time as Little American." My goose bumps weren't going away.

"Let's get out of here," I said. I swept the light back up the tunnel and started back out. Dylan didn't say a word as we headed back. I couldn't tell if he was deep in thought or disappointed.

We passed the tunnel fork, and I was about to say something when I heard a crunch. "Shh, listen," I whispered. "I think someone's coming." It was quiet, but the sound of hard footsteps began to echo in the mine.

I grabbed Dylan's arm and yanked hard towards the first tunnel. My flashlight beam found a rock niche, and we both crammed in. A soft click cuts off Dylan's flashlight and mine followed. Around the edge of the rocks, we watched a bouncing flashlight beam and heard heavy breathing. The flashlight caught some glassy quartz on the wall and reflected back. A guy in a dark-green park uniform with a pickaxe slung over his shoulder was walking right for us.

I jerked Dylan out of the beam of light and held my breath as the footsteps came closer and closer.

"Crap," Dylan barely whispered. The cold wall of the mine numbed my back. We were plastered tight against the wall. If he came down the right side of the mine, we would be found. The footsteps stopped just where the tunnel split. The flashlight beam shone down the shaft just missing us. The rock wall was biting into my back. For once I was glad I was small and skinny. I disappeared into the wall, but Dylan did not. The guy stood there what felt like an hour. Slowly, the beam of light shone past us. I willed myself not to move and held my breath. Far away, a soft whistle was coming from the mine entrance where the wind blew across the opening. The mine was painfully quiet.

Suddenly the light was gone. We heard the footsteps going down the left side of the mine. I counted to ten, grabbed Dylan's shirt tugging him towards the entrance. I turned on my flashlight. We raced up the tunnel towards the mine entrance. Deep in the mine, we heard the ring of a pick-axe.

Tumbling through the mine barrier, our eyes squinted at the sun, trying to adjust to the light. I made my way for the trail back to the boat. When I looked back, Dylan was gone.

"Let's go." I heard a muffled call. Dylan had gone off trail. I spotted him through a wall of green. Pushing my way through the brush with only a few bleeding scratches, Dylan pointed to narrow deer path. "We will circle off trail and head back down to the boat."

"Why can't we just take the trail?" I asked.

"We really shouldn't have been there," he whispered. He glanced back to the mine shaft, but then followed the skinny deer trail.

"He doesn't know that," I replied and pushed tree boughs out of the way.

"Yeah, I know but I don't think he's going to care." Dylan was moving at a good clip. He led the way, darting around the trees. He picked up speed and ran faster down the slope, dodging tree branches and prickly bushes to the lake shore. I stumbled after him bumping into boulders and sharp brush.

"Why?" I jumped and slid around the rocks trying not to fall. Despite his size, Dylan was nimble.

He was at a full run by the time we reached the dock. He yanked the ropes off the mooring, tossing them into the boat. "Get in," he urgently said. "I'll push off."

I barely had time to sit down when Dylan shoved us away from the dock. I struggled with my life jacket as he jumped in and grabbed an oar. He quickly paddled for a good dozen strokes before he tried to crank the motor.

"What's going on?" I asked. Nervous, Dylan kept searching the shoreline. I looked back at the shore and said, "I don't think he'd throw us in jail for ducking under a rope."

"A real park ranger wouldn't," Dylan stated.

"A real park ranger?" I questioned.

"Yeah, first, park rangers don't use canoes to check their park sites. The park has really nice boats with dual 250-horsepower outboards. You can hear them coming."

I then noticed a canoe hidden up along the shore close to the dock. "Second," my cousin continued, "they usually don't carry guns." I hadn't even noticed that the ranger was carrying a gun. The motor sputtered to life as Dylan turned the boat back to the cabin. Over the roar of the motor, Dylan shouted out, "That was no park ranger."

I searched the shoreline, but the guy didn't appear. Little American Island disappeared as we followed the buoys back to the cabin. Night was falling when we anchored the boat to the dock. The haunting calls of the checkered loons began as the night came.

Three

MORNINGS WERE EARLY UP NORTH. A loud scream made me jump a foot off the bed. I didn't bother to get up. A bald eagle sat lookout on the white pine outside my window. He was an old friend and always shrieked as dawn appeared. I stared at him from my blankets as he guarded the lake. A fully mature eagle, he was almost as big as me with white head and tail feathers, yellow beak and a black-brown body. The tree was his early morning roost for breakfast. Something caught his eye and wings flared. He gracefully lifted from the tree and flew out over the lake.

I barrel rolled the blankets around me for a longer snooze, but my nose picked up bacon cooking. I reversed the roll, dumping myself out of bed. My clothes were still in a pile at the top of the stairs. I searched for something to wear. After we got back from Little American, the night was filled with my uncle chatting and outlining the rules of the house. Again the basics, don't get yourself killed or kill your cousin and pick up your stuff, seemed fair to me. The same clothes that I had on the night before were handy, so I got dressed and went downstairs.

Uncle Mike had talked the whole evening, so Dylan and I didn't have time to discuss what happened on Little American. My aunt was staying with my folks for the summer doing an engineering job. It was only us. Uncle Mike divided the chores in three categories, yard, house, and cooking. The three of us would rotate through the chores weekly. Uncle Mike was cooking this week, just to show us easy stuff. I had the yard work while Dylan had house cleaning.

Dylan was already in the kitchen standing at the stove. Uncle Mike was showing him how to burn bacon. "Turn the heat up really high and then ignore it. It gets that nice black coloring." Shells were breaking as Uncle Mike cracked eggs into a fry pan. Dylan pulled the still golden brown bacon out of the pan to drain on a plate.

"Hey, Henry, sleep okay?" Uncle Mike chimed.

"Yep. The eagle is pretty loud in the morning."

The plate full of bacon thumped on the table. Dylan pulled orange juice from the fridge. "He's really annoying," he griped.

"Can't oversleep out here. You like your eggs sunny side up?" Uncle Mike asked.

"Sure," I answered and grabbed some plates and forks.

"Good, b'cuz that's the only way I do 'em," he said as he slid two eggs and several pieces of bacon on a plate. He pointed to the toaster with his spatula. I reached over and pulled the toast out.

Plates were full as we sat at the small table in the kitchen. Uncle Mike crunched into a piece of bacon and nosily chewed, "So what's up for today?"

"First, our chores," I said, might as well rack up some points with Uncle Mike.

Dylan rolled his eyes. "Suck up," he mouthed.

"Then I thought we could do some fishing," I added and Dylan perked up.

"Sounds good, but you need to head over to the store to get a fishing license before you put a line in the water. I already registered you with Customs so if you guys accidently cross over to the Canada side, I won't have to jail you." Uncle Mike wiped his plate clean with the last bit of toast. "I hate all that paper work." He popped the toast in his mouth. "I'm in the office today, so I expect to be home on time. Burgers okay for tonight?" We both grunted as he pulled his uniform cap on and headed for the door. "Of course, I'd rather have fish. That's if you guys can hook anything," he challenged and walked out the door.

Silence stilled the air for a moment as we looked at each other and then scrambled. "Fill a pot of water to boil for the dishes. I'll get started," I said. Dylan was already piling dirty dishes into the sink.

It didn't take long, and we were on our bikes heading for the Last Stop. The grocery, bait and license shop was the last bit of civilization on the edge of the wilderness. We always went every summer to buy supplies, gas, fresh chubs or shiners for bait and to inhale the best homemade ice cream in the world. The family store, along with the secret ice cream recipe, had existed since people started to come to the lake.

We biked on a winding, rolling dirt road with soft green pines and tamaracks hugging the road. Puffy clouds were stacked high in the blue sky. Small rocks popped out from under our tires as we scared deer at the side of the road. A fat raccoon crossed the road in front of us.

"The fake ranger. You know him?" I asked.

"Nobody, I know," Dylan replied. "Not a townie. I know everyone that lives here." It's a small town. Uncle Mike and Dylan know just about everyone.

"It's pretty stupid to dress up like park ranger. Dad would shred him if he caught 'em."

"Are you gonna tell him?" I asked.

"Naw, we'd have to confess. We would get into trouble for being there." We dodged pot holes and divots. "Dad would probably shred us."

I had no doubt that he would. I was thinking about it when Dylan launched into a detail conversation if we should get shiners or chubs. Shiners were bait fish used in the spring with sparkly silver sides. Chubs were darker and used in the summer. The problem was that it was a late spring and was being slow to warm up for summer. I was pushing for chubs while Dylan claimed it was still spring because of the ice going out on the lake so late. I was ready to agree when I saw her waiting for us in front of the Last Stop.

Four

I DON'T REMEMBER MEETING ARLA. When I thought of summers at the lake, I first thought of Dylan and then Arla. The same age as us, she lived with her grandmother, Gammy Mary, her only relative. At thirteen, Arla ran the store better than most adults. The store would be hers, but she was racing a clock. Gammy was in her eighties and wouldn't be around forever. Arla had been in a hurry to grow up for as long as I'd known her.

"'Bout time, Henry," she said as we coasted up to the store. She now equaled Dylan's height, but half his bulk. Her dark hair hung stick straight down her back almost to her waist, but that was not what held my eye. My mom claimed her eyes were cornflower blue. I didn't even know what a cornflower was, but Arla's blue eyes are the color of the early morning sky.

"Hey, Arla, I'm here for the summer," I replied.

"I heard. You ready for blistering hot summer days of seventy-five degrees and pathetic company?" She shot a grin over to Dylan.

"Oh, Arla," Dylan teased, "You're hurting me. Besides you shouldn't get so down on yourself."

"You're so right, Dylan. I'm just going to shrivel up and die of embarrassment," she kidded and then paused to grin, "but only when I'm around you knuckleheads."

"Hey," I butted in. Arla and Dylan could annoy each other all day, but I wanted to go fishing. "How 'bout a fishing license and some bait?"

She reached for the bait bucket that dangled from Dylan's handlebars. "So what's it going to be, shiners or chubs?" She gave Dylan a smirk, "Don't take his advice. He still needs help baiting his own hook."

"Shiners," I decided.

"Good choice. That's what they're biting on," with the bucket in hand she headed back into the store.

"You always say that," I yelled. "What would you say if I'd said chubs?" We parked our bikes and followed her in.

"Good choice. That's what their biting on," she laughed as I stepped into the mystery of the Last Stop. While Arla reached for a plastic pitcher to scoop up the bait, I took a good look around.

The shop catered to the seasons that rotated from fisherman to hunters, then snowmobilers. One could pick out shiners, chubs, leaches, or minnows from the giant glass bins that bubbled air through cold water. Rods, tackle jigs and spinners, nets or dock bumper guards crammed the shelves. Life jackets and inner tubes hung from the ceiling along with a rack of rope and chains. Basic groceries were on the other side of the store. Fresh milk or pop was in the refrigerated unit, but the groceries leaned heavily on the fish fry mix and chips. A first aid section had kits to help pull out fish hooks or deal with poison ivy right next to the rack of flip-flops. By the register, a small grill counter could cook up a hot dog or burger. Right next to the grill nestled the freezer with the secret recipe ice cream. There were no specialty flavors here, just chocolate, vanilla, and strawberry . . . maybe. The aisles were narrow and shelving high. Gammy Mary was sitting behind the cash register with the license application already ready for me.

"Henry, I heard you're here for the whole summer." Gammy was like those tough stunted pines that clung to life on windblown islands. She had weathered winters that regularly saw minus forty below. Her tiny frame was propped up on a stool and as always, her steel gray hair was pulled back into a tidy bun. She gave me a once-over look with those cornflower-blue eyes. A bit faded, but they were still clear as she fixed her gaze on me. "You haven't changed at all, have ya?"

"No, ma'am." I guess that was a polite way of telling me that I hadn't grown an inch.

Arla dipped the pitcher into the shiner tank. "You want one or two scoops?" she asked.

"Just one scoop," I said while grabbing my wallet. "We can get our limit of walleye with a dozen. I don't want to feed the fish." I forked out the money for the license and shiners. Arla dumped two healthy scoops of shiners in a plastic bag. She blasted some oxygen in the bag and gave it a quick twist and closed it with a rubber band.

"If it was just you, Henry, a dozen would do, but you've got Dylan with you."

"Tough talking, Arla. Gammy, can you do without 'worthless' here for a few hours?" Dylan nodded towards Arla, who was grinning.

Arla shrugged, "Pete knows enough now to run the place. He's coming in soon, so you can have lunch. He always wants a few more hours."

"She needs a fishing lesson," Dylan sighed. "Best she comes with us so she can learn something. Of course, she's probably too much of a girl to get her hands dirty. Maybe she should stay here and work instead of going out with the pros." He picked up the plastic bag of shiners and peered into the bag. A swarm of shiny sided minnows crowded the bag. He tucked them into the bait bucket and headed for the door.

"Big talk, Dylan Wilder," Arla winked at Gammy. "I'll be back with supper. It shouldn't take that long. That is if Dylan's boat doesn't sink." Her fishing gear and windbreaker were already stashed behind the front door. She had this all planned as I followed her outside.

Walleye are the Cadillac of fish. Dylan and Arla wouldn't eat anything else. Small mouth bass were too mushy. Northern pike had those pesky Y bones. Largemouth bass were okay, but weren't easy to find in Rainy Lake. Perch and bluegill had too many bones. Only the walleye put up a challenge to get caught, but then lay like wet dish rags once they were on the hook. They melted in your mouth, and a guy could get his limit in one hour or fish the whole day and get nothing. Today was a good day.

We ended up using all the shiners. They were biting hard and after measuring and releasing the walleye that weren't the right size—we couldn't keep a walleye between seventeen and twenty-eight inches—we had to toss them back in so they made little walleye, we had our limit of four walleye each. Two hours after we left the dock, we were back and in the boat house filleting twelve fish.

Dylan could fillet and talk at the same time. He sliced off the fins, ran a thin sharp blade right behind the gills. His knife ran down the spine, separating flesh from spine. He picked up the half and pretended to take a chomp out of it.

"Hey, did you hear the one about the fishermen who decides to eat sushi?" he started. It was one of his favorite stories. Arla was already rolling her eyes. Uncle Mike had told us the tale a few years back and I'd rather forget it.

"Tell us and then I don't want to hear it again the entire summer," she muttered. Dylan had to tell this story at least once every summer.

"Okay, so these fishermen decide to eat raw lake fish, probably perch since they're too dumb to get nice walleye like this." Concentrating, he flipped the slab of fish, skin side down and ran his knife under the ridge of bones. Loosening the ribs with his knife tip, he pulled the ribs off with his other hand.

"They like sushi and so since they're camping up the Seine River in the upper arm of Rainy, they decide to make a meal of fresh fish." His fingers sought the edge of the fish half. Carefully, he slid the knife against the skin peeling the fillet off. He held up a white translucent slab of fish and his eyes got a bit glassy.

"There's a nice fillet," he whispered and began again. "So they make a meal of raw fish eating till their bellies were full." He flipped the fish over and started on the other side.

"They didn't think too much more of it until they went home. Weeks later they noticed their bellies were swelling up. Thought they were getting fat." He slid another fillet onto the plate and grabbed another fish.

"About a month later, one of them went for some really spicy Mexican food." Dylan slid another fillet onto the plate. "The guy really loves those hot jalapeno peppers and he must've popped a dozen or more down." Dylan was already finished with that fish and was reaching for another.

"Before he knew it, he's having a terrible belly ache and had to go take a crap."

This was the part of the story that Dylan liked the best. I was starting to smile at how much Dylan was enjoying it. Arla was picking at her fingernails sitting on a stool looking totally bored.

"He goes to the john," Dylan started to laugh really loud, "and chunks of stuff come out. He doesn't know what it is until he's staring in the toilet and realizes it's part of one big worm."

"Idiot, didn't know that you have to cook freshwater fish. Perch can have those tapeworms." He was laughing and filleting, flinging his knife around. I just stayed out of the way of his knife.

"Never heard that one before, Dylan," I laughed and Arla gave in and let out a quick chuckle.

"No? Let it be a lesson then," he said. He sounded so much like his dad I really laughed and Arla joined in. We were sitting in the boathouse laughing together, and I realized the summer would go by way too fast.

Arla would take her perfect eight boneless fillets home, but ours wouldn't last the night. Uncle Mike would fry them in beer batter as fast as we could eat them. We placed all the fillets in the fridge and decided to find the Monopoly game to fill the time before Uncle Mike got home.

"Did you see it on the closet shelf, Henry?" Dylan asked as he plodded upstairs. My bag was sitting right where I had left it the night before, and before I could answer, Dylan tripped over it. He lost his balance and crashed right through the thin wall into the skeleton of the rafters.

I bit my lip to keep from laughing. The big guy went down really hard. I reached out a hand to help him up, "Sorry, Dylan. Anything hurt? That is besides the wall." I sniggered. Arla was tugging on his shirt to help him out. A Dylan size hole was punched in the wall. A little triangle of space was exposed between the wall of the attic room and the roof. It was just big enough for a person to sit. Dylan was unhurt, but Arla and I stuck our heads in to look around. The cabin was never meant as a winter home so there was no insulation, only bare log rafters and dust. I started sneezing.

I pulled the neckline of my t-shirt over my nose. "I think I can fit," I said and scooted in under the roof. Dust stirred up as I crawled. The ventilation holes under the roof line were big enough to bounce in light. It was dead space, the air hot and lifeless. I saw nothing until I reached the last rafter. At first, I thought it was a part of the floor. Just a lump tightly jammed between two floor joists. It was a small dusty packet wrapped in old newspaper tied with string. As I picked it up, I sneezed loudly and sent a cloud of dust everywhere. There was no room to turn around so I grasped the packet and slowly backed up.

"Hey, I found something," I said. "It's the only thing here except for the dust." Arla took the packet while Dylan yanked me out. Arla laughed at me. Cobwebs and dust balls hung off my hair and clothes. She gave a quick swipe to get the worst off, and we stared at the package.

It was small, perhaps three-by-five inches and felt like a slim book. The newspaper was old. Carefully, Arla pulled the string snugged around the book so long it fell apart. The newspaper had yellowed and began to flake off in fragile pieces. Arla carefully peeled back the sheets.

"Look," she held up a section of the paper. "It's the *International Falls Daily Journal*." We could just make out enough of the letters to confirm it was the local newspaper. "It's from July 21, 1931." Large pieces of newspaper fell away as she exposed a small black leather-bound book.

"It's pretty old. Look, the back is creased and the finish on the leather is scuffed up," I said as Dylan squeezed me out of my spot.

"Quit shoving, Dylan. Let's move it over to the table by the window. Arla, you sit in the middle so we all can see," I suggested.

"Okay and let's move everything so they don't get crushed," said Arla.

We picked up the fragments and hauled them carefully over, setting them to the side. Arla waited until the chairs were pressed close and then opened the book. The pages were stained yellow and the ink was a faded brown. "It's a journal of some sort. The first page is dated May 28, 1931." Her finger traced the letters lightly.

Dylan was squinting, "Can you read it?"

The writing was small, but legible as Arla began.

Five

May 28, 1931, International Falls, Minnesota

I'm sitting on Blood Rock waiting for my best friend, O.C. The waves are pounding the shore. My coat is buttoned up to my ears. Rainy Lake is playing with the Canadian wind, pushing up white caps as high as my knees. I tuck my chin deep into my coat collar trying to keep the wind out. Eighth-grade graduation was today, but I'll probably never get to high school.

My dad has been gone the whole winter now. That's not good. He went to work as a lumberjack in one of the timber camps, but the spring thaw was weeks ago, and he hasn't shown up. I'm afraid that he got crushed by the logs or trapped in the woods and froze. No way of telling.

We've been getting by with O.C. and me finding bottles and selling them to the moonshiners. They always need bottles for the corn liquor. I get five cents a bottle and can make a dollar or two. Mom makes some money, taking in laundry and sewing, but it seems like my belly is always grinding against my backbone.

My behind is getting numb from sitting on this rock. Blood Rock has been here forever. Someone spilled red paint on it long ago. Most of the red is gone, but some of the paint still sits in the cracks. I tell my little sisters the rock is stained red from chopped off heads. I grab one under each arm and pretend that I'm taking them to the rock. They get all scared and scream, but then I wink at them and they laugh.

Here comes O.C's boat. He's got a pretty little sixteen-footer with a fifteen-horsepower motor that acts like thirty. O.C. stands for Oil Can and he's skinny as a twig. He has a real name but won't tell anyone, not even me. He did fourth grade twice, and he doesn't want to go back to school. His real job is tinkering with engines. He can make anything run and loves a sputtering motor. Oil has soaked into his hands and nail beds. He'll never get them clean and now instead of Oil Can, everyone calls him O.C.

He lives with his dad and baby sister. His mom died during birthing. It was real sad, but his dad found an old Indian woman to take care of the baby while he works the store. On the outskirts of town, their place is more a tarpaper shack than a store. They sell eggs, milk, and garden vegetables. During fishing season he has a horse trough covered with boards, where you can buy bait minnows. The garage is attached, where O.C. sells gas or fixes car or boat engines. Right behind their place is a caged bear that they charge a dime for the tourist to see. The bear is so old, he's toothless with patches of his black fur falling out leaving him bald in places, but the tourists don't care. They'll spend money on anything even a blind pig.

That's how O.C.'s dad makes his real money. He has a pig that he claims is sightless. The pig looks like he can see just fine. O.C.'s dad charges a whole dollar to see him and as the folks stare at the pig that looks perfectly normal, O.C.'s dad offers them a bit of refreshment, usually his first rate moonshine that he makes in a still in the back woods. Prohibition is the law and having a speakeasy bar and selling alcohol is illegal. A lot of people brew moonshine to sell to the Chicago crooks that come up just to buy booze.

Canada is on the other side of the lake and alcohol is still legal there. At night you can sit right here on Blood Rock and watch men try to haul Canadian whisky across Rainy Lake. They almost always get caught by the law before they reach shore. The moonshine is local and cheap, but the Canadian whiskey gets top dollar. It's big money.

O. C. is landing his boat.

Arla paused as we heard Uncle Mike's truck. Carefully thumbing through the pages she said, "It's a journal. He's coming out of the eighth grade, maybe he's around fourteen, just a year older than us." We heard Uncle Mike calling for us downstairs.

Dylan reached over and closed the book in Arla's hands. "Hey, Dad," he yelled out. "Look in the fridge." He pushed the book into the center of the table and whispered, "No one looks at the book till we all get back together."

Arla's hands twitched wanting to open it again, "But who is he? I could bring it home and search through it."

"Tomorrow," I said and stood up to go downstairs.

Arla tugged her dark hair behind her ears and pushed herself up, "Okay, but no peeking. I should be getting back to Gammy. Tomorrow, I'll meet you pass Steamboat Island, and then we can go to my island for shore lunch," she said as we made our way down to see Uncle Mike.

Shore lunch meant we were going fishing. Steamboat was an island that, in profile, looked like a boat chugging across the lake. On the east side was a little island called Walleye Island. I didn't think that was the real name of the island, but we caught so many walleye there, that was our name for it now. It would be good fishing this time of year, and we could hook three or four fish and then fry them up for lunch at the island.

The shore lunch island was Arla's. She owned the entire island. When her folks died in a boating accident, it became hers. The island had been in the family for years. Gammy made sure Arla owned it legally. She even paid taxes. Many had offered her big bucks for it, but she wouldn't sell. She's crazy about the place and for now, it only had a campsite on it, but Arla claimed that one day she'd build a home there.

Uncle Mike was pulling out the big fry pan. He placed it on the stove on high. He had a big grin on his face and gave Arla a hug big enough to make her squeak. "Now this makes sense," he said. He pointed to the pile of fillets all ready to be dredged in cracker crumbs, salt, and pepper. "Arla, you did all the catching while the guys sat and did nothing?"

"Naw," she laughed, "Anyone could've caught fish today. They were jumping in the boat. I'm just glad Dylan didn't sink us before we got out of the bay." She pulled her packet of fillets out of the fridge. "I need to get these home so Gammy and I can eat."

"I can run you home, Arla." Uncle Mike was pouring oil into the heated pan, but stopped and wiped his hands on his pants.

"Thanks but no. Got my bike here. Won't take me long to get home. See you guys tomorrow around ten. I'll bring the shiners this time." She smiled at us as she went out the door, "Glad you finally made it here, Henry," she called out.

"That girl can fish," Uncle Mike said as the first fillet slid into the hot pan with a hard sizzle. The heavenly scent of fresh fish filled the air. "Where did you guys go?"

"Out by milepost marker number three," said Dylan as he pulled out plates. It's a buoy marker to warn boaters of a cluster of rocks and one of the favorite places to fish on Rainy.

"Arla's right," I added. "The fish were begging to get caught today." It was fun to be out in the boat and reeling in fish, but the journal was pulling at me. The year 1931 would be towards the end of prohibition period.

"Uncle Mike, was there a lot of bootlegging up here during Prohibition?" I searched for some raw carrots, broccoli and ranch dressing. By the time I washed the vegetables. Uncle Mike placed a plateful of golden fillets on the table. We all sat down quick and piled our plates high.

Uncle Mike took a forkful of fish and let out a steady hum. He finally said, "This brings tears to my eyes. It is amazing. Always is at the beginning of the summer."

I took my first bite of the season. It was miraculous. The walleye flaked and melted in my mouth. I shoved another bite in as Uncle Mike began.

"Making, selling and stealing liquor was a way of life up here. It was hard to make a living by fishing or farming during that time period. A few became rich by the timber trade. The tourist trade was slow back then. Not everyone, but quite a few had stills to make moonshine or corn liquor. Al Capone and Baby Face Nelson would come up this way to buy and transport the liquor back to Chicago." He paused to take another bite of walleye.

"Al Capone and Baby Face Nelson were Chicago mobsters?" I asked.

"Al Capone had a cabin up on Crowe Lake. He didn't show up often though. Chicago's St. Valentine Massacre had just happened, killing seven members of the Bugs Moran gang. Everyone thought Capone had done it, and he was lying low. The local newspaper reported an eyewitness account that Baby Face Nelson was showing up at church on Sundays. Lots of people became rich hauling and selling liquor. I'm sure all the crime lords made their way up here."

He pointed his fork at the kitchen window that looked out over the lake. The Canadian shore was visible enough to see small specks of cars moving on the coastal highway. "It was Canada that drew them all here. They'd run boats across the lake almost from anywhere to a pickup point and would load up with Canadian whiskey. Some boats never made it. Too loaded down with liquor. They'd sink in bad weather and high waves. However, it was worth the risk. People could make more money in one run than they could make in a year. Those were hard times. The nation was coming out of the Depression. It was hard living up here."

"Dad, wasn't the cabin built during that time?" Dylan grabbed the last fish fillet from the platter. I was too stuffed to fight him for it.

"Don't know for sure but I have a feeling it was built in the early 1930s. I remodeled one of the bedrooms a few years back and found newspapers stuffed in the wall from the 1930s. Still have them somewhere." He pushed himself away from the table. "Guys, good thing you had Arla along to help."

"She didn't help that much," I blurted out. "I mean, she caught her share. We're going again tomorrow."

Uncle Mike laughed, "Good. Just make sure you take her."

I opened my mouth to add a comment when Dylan gave me a hard look to shut up. "We're going out past Steamboat Island," he quickly said.

I got the impression he didn't want me to say that we were going to Arla's island. I kept my mouth shut and just nodded.

"A bit early this time of year, but give it a try. Since you guys brought in the fish. I'll do the dishes."

We scrambled to clear the table, and when we carried the last dish over, I asked Dylan. "My line has some kinks. Can you help me straighten it out?" He got the hint right away and soon we're out the door and headed for the boathouse.

We're almost to the boat house when I asked, "So what's wrong with telling Uncle Mike that we're going to Arla's island?"

"Really nothing, he knows we go out there. He just thinks we're going to fall and break our necks or something. Either way he always wants us to have an adult with us. That's hard since Gammy doesn't get out to the island very much anymore and Dad's just too busy. But I really didn't want you to tell him about the journal, at least not yet."

I wanted to know who wrote it and why the book had been hidden in the rafters of this cabin. "Let's read tonight and see if we can find out anything else."

Dylan walked into the boathouse. "One, we promised to read it together and two, if Arla finds out . . ." he gave an involuntary shudder. He reached up to grab my fishing rod off the boathouse wall, "and she will find out. She knows when I'm lying."

"Now, there's nothing wrong with this thing," he said. He gave the line a hard pull and searched for a knot.

"Naw," I answered. "I just wanted to get you out of the house so we could talk."

"Henry, you've got to learn to lie a bit better. You know Dad keeps all this gear in prime shape. He went over it himself just before you got up here. Next time pick out an excuse that's believable." He rolled in the line and placed the rod back up onto the wall. Dylan then laughed, "like how to tie a hook on, or cast a line, or hook a shiner."

"Okay, I got the point. I did get three fish today."

"Yeah, but we threw back two because they were too small. You just didn't see Arla slip two of hers onto your stringer."

"Oh." I felt my shoulders slump down.

"Hey, don't feel bad. You're already much better than you were last year. By the end of the summer you'll be slipping walleye over to her." Dylan slapped me hard on my back to cheer me up, but it stung.

Uncle Mike wandered down to the dock to ask about the line. I quickly confessed that it must have been my casting skills and not the line. Dylan grinned with approval. It wasn't really a lie, but the confession caused a two-hour lesson on casting off the end of the deck. My arm ached by the time the sun was starting to set.

Zonked, I was ready to go to bed. As I climbed up the stairs, I made up my mind to cheat and look at the book. Arla would never know. I wanted to figure out the writer. Heading right for the table, I searched the tabletop where we all took the promise, but the book was gone.

Six

I RAN DOWNSTAIRS TO TELL DYLAN. Wrapped in blankets, he was examining a Lund boat brochure, daydreaming about something new and fast. He laughed, "That sneaky Arla. She must've grabbed it before she left. She doesn't trust us at all. I bet she's reading the whole thing right now."

I was mad. Just because I was going to do the exact same thing didn't cross my mind. I flopped down on Dylan's bed. "What if someone else grabbed it?"

"Henry, our closest neighbor's a mile away, and I don't think a bird or critter came in to get it. Calm down. She has it and she's going to gloat about it as soon as she sees us."

"Well, we shouldn't tell her about the gold," I declared.

"She knows. She was the one that told me. We can toss her in the water tomorrow if that would make you feel better," said Dylan. "Get some sleep and we'll think of revenge tomorrow."

"After we get the book," I muttered.

Dylan shoved the brochure at me. "Do you think a ninety-horsepower, four-stroke Merc is too much power for my boat?"

I took a quick look at the motor. "Yes, too big and too heavy," I stated. The motor would sink his boat before he could leave the dock.

"Dang, forgot about the weight," he said taking his brochure back as I took off for bed again.

Arla arrived at Walleye Island just as we were setting up our rods. She has a sixteen-footer with a twenty-five horsepower motor that had belonged to her parents. She sided up to us to lash the boats together. Our boats bobbed up and down out of synch until we tied them at the bow and stern. They rolled together over the waves. Dylan cushioned the boat edges with torpedo shaped bumpers. Arla looked distracted today. Her brow furrowed as she pulled a fishing cap down low to keep her hair out of her eyes.

Dylan stared at her for a moment and then asked, "What's up?"

She immediately began, "The freezer unit's being cranky. I'm probably going to have to buy a new one. I have to decide if selling the ice cream is worth it. The grocer's complaining about the increase in fuel and wants to slap on a fuel surcharge for delivery. The economy sucks, and Gammy didn't look good this morning," she said all in one breath.

"She okay?" Dylan delicately asked.

Arla shrugged, "As best as can be expected. She starts fussing over the store stuff, and then I can see her shift her worrying about me. The store doesn't make all that much money and all that worrying is awfully hard on her."

I guess I won't be giving her a bad time about taking the book. She had enough to worry about. "Do you need to get back? We can always go fishing another day," I suggested.

"No. Gammy loved the fish last night, and I just have to get back to handle the second shift. I'm good till about 2:00 p.m. We just need to start getting those fish on the line." She handed us a bucket of shiners, and we hooked them through the mouth and just below the fin for trolling. Arla dropped her trolling motor, and we started a slow ride along the shore.

We just got settled when Dylan pulled in his first walleye. It was almost sixteen inches, a real beauty, and he slipped the fish onto a stringer and over the edge of the boat. My mouth watered remembering last night's dinner when Dylan asked, "How about we fish for a couple of hours, and then head over to the island? Do a shore lunch, and then you can get back home, Arla."

Her head nodded as she stared across the lake, not really paying attention to her line or us. "Hey, Arla, read anything good last night?" I asked.

A slow smirk pulled her out of her dark thoughts. "I was busy working under the freezer unit and staring at the mess that's the cooling unit."

I noticed the scratches on her arms and hands from her machine encounter as she reached inside a sack and pulled out the journal.

"Right. So how much did you read?" I asked.

She gave me a quizzical look that reeked of guilt, "Some of it. I was too busy to read it all. Then I forgot that I put it under the cash register. I had to go back to get it this morning."

We were about a hundred feet from a tree-lined shore right past a ridge of rocks that sat thirty feet below the water. Reaching over to shut off the trolling motor, she said, "Dylan, throw out that anchor and use some of that savvy fishing skill you always brag about to bring a few more in." She cushioned her head with an extra lifejacket and stretched her legs out. A slight breeze cooled the hard sunshine as the waves gently bobbed the boats up and down. She opened the book and cleared her throat.

May 30, 1931

O.C. and I made a killing last night. The lumberjacks come out of the woods after being snowed in all winter and spent all their money getting drunk. They buy bottles of moonshine and go down to watch the water go over the dam. The empty bottles get tossed into the Rainy River and float downstream. We found a pile of bottles down by the landing up from the Rainy River dam. We scrubbed them up a bit and sold them all to O.C.'s dad. I was able to give 85 cents to my mom. We had chicken and dumplings for dinner for the first time in months. My stomach still aches from being full.

I'm watching O.C. work at his dad's shop. He's tinkering on a 1929 Ford Tudor Sedan. O.C. was doing a special. It was being used for bootlegging liquor from the border to Chicago but the federal officers, the feds, are onto the bootleggers. They'll stop a car if it looks loaded down with liquor, so O.C.'s doing his magic. He was adding extra heavy duty springs and suspensions to the car so even loaded down with liquor, it would ride like an empty car. O.C. is really good at fixing cars.

"Who do you think this car belongs to?" he asked from underneath the front wheel.

The car was gorgeous. Black and sleek, designed for speed and yet not flashy, "No one from around here," I replied. If you were lucky enough to have a car, it would be a truck, something to haul wood or work the farm. My hand ran over the sleekness of the hood. I wanted one.

"It's Ogaard's," he answered as he came out from under the car.

I was shocked, "You're giving me a line." Ogaard was dirt poor and lived out by Roger's Corner just before you hit town. He had been trying to farm on 80 acres of rock, clay and bog for as long as I've known him. He gave up trying to grow a crop and had moved on to cows that got hoof rot from the wet muskeg to sheep that were starving.

"It's on the up and up," O.C. claimed.

"If so, is he making or taking?"

"Both from what I heard," O.C. said and stood up wiping his hands on an old rag. "He gets his corn from someone that actually knows how to grow it and then makes some powerful corn liquor. He's got some type of fancy still that can make almost pure alcohol. He then drives to Chicago and delivers it himself." O.C. wipes the wheel hub and shines the rim. "But that's not how he got the car."

"Okay, I'll take the bait. How did he get the car?" I asked.

"Al Capone."

I stared at him in disbelief. How did a clay scratching farmer get a car from Al Capone? "Naw, don't believe it."

"It's true. The deal is that he only sells to Capone and Capone lets him have the car."

I'm staring at the car and wondering how I can get such a deal.

"Uncle Mike claims that big crime lords would come up here to deal for any type of booze, but it sounds like Al Capone was trying to corner the market. I bet a lot of people got whacked over a bad deal," I said. I was half asleep lying across the gently rocking boat watching a few ducks fly overhead.

"I wonder how many people made moonshine during that time?" pondered Dylan.

Arla replied, "Probably a lot did for their own use, most people would be afraid of getting caught by the law. The speakeasies of the big cities probably paid off the police or feds. Corruption was big back then." Arla looked up as Dylan pulled up another walleye. She snapped the book closed and started to unhook the boats.

"Henry, I think you have a fish on your line."

My line was pulling hard, but I was thinking about O.C. and who wrote the journal. The rod almost pulled out of my hands. I jerked hard on the line. Dylan shouted out. "Easy, walleye have soft mouths. You can pull the hook right out of them."

I eased up and started rolling the line in. Dylan swooped down with a net and scooped my fish right as it broke the surface. I stuck my fingers right behind the gills and measured it on the ruler pasted on the inside of the boat. "It's a keeper, thirteen inches almost fourteen." Dylan gave me a thumb's up. He had already pulled up the stringer with three walleye. Somehow Dylan had managed to get three fish while I was listening. "I'll cook," I volunteered.

Arla really laughed and said, "No way. You can find the wood and do clean up. You forgot what happened the last time you tried to cook?"

"That was last year and the fish were still good. You just had to eat around the burnt parts."

"Henry, I don't forgive easily, especially when it comes to torching walleye," said Arla. "Your Uncle Mike should've arrested you."

Just because we hadn't caught any for a week didn't mean they had to hate me for it.

"You can make it up this year by staying away from the cooking," Arla added.

"Okay, okay, I get it. I'll clean up." I put the rods down and made sure the stringer of fish and bait bucket were back in the boat.

Dylan was checking on Arla. She gave him an "I'm good" nod. They both started up their motors, and we turned west towards Arla's island. Arla never named her island. I'm not even sure it was on a map. Whenever I asked her about it, she claimed she would someday but just couldn't come up with a name special enough yet.

We motored by Bushyhead Island and spotted the eagle's nest. A pair of eagles had nested there forever. It was good to see them again. I saw at least two eaglets all covered in pale fuzz. Soon they'd stand on the edge of their nest testing their wings. We passed the nest and heard the high pitch screech of one of the parents, just warning us to keep away.

We turned north towards Arla's island. The wind had picked up a bit making the waves higher. Cold water spray stung my face. Everything up here felt more. The sky was bluer. The clouds were thicker. The trees stood greener with the air alive with the scent of trees, water, and sky. The wind was blowing my hair back, my face was soaked. I was happy.

The boats crunched on the sandy bay on the south side of Arla's island. We anchored both boats to a solitary rock. A grove of white pines, a hundred years old towered on the island. They were all stunted at the top. White pine weevils had damaged the tops years ago and a lot of aged white pines had the characteristic lopped off look.

Most of the island's shore was aged granite making the shore hard to land except at the sand beach. She had a small camp site already set up. A good fire burned by the time I brought back more firewood. Dylan had all the fillets piled high on a tin plate and Arla took out a bag of flour and seasoning from her backpack. The fire took hold and Arla placed an old iron rack over the flames. A heavy cast iron fry pan went on top. The oil was poured and when it started to shimmer, the fillets went in. They were so fresh, they curled in the pan. We all stared as they turned a golden brown. Arla slid three filets onto a plate for Dylan and two onto hers. She wrinkled her nose in mock disgust, "You want me to burn these a bit, Henry?"

I shoved a plate at her as she slid the last three fillets on my plate. I grabbed a good spot on a log and stared at the fish. I knew it was sizzling hot. I didn't care. The fillet bounced back and forth between my fingers until I could give it a good pull, steam floated up fragrant with salt and pepper. Portions of flaky fish popped into my mouth. It sizzled in my mouth and my fingers burned. It was so good. We ate fast, burning our mouths. Almost always we napped afterwards, our bellies full and the sun warm. We would snooze for an hour or two, but not today. Arla had to get back to help out, but for now she wasn't thinking about the store. Dylan and I were still juggling our hot fish as she went down to the shore to rinse off her plate and hands. Setting her plate out to dry, she wiped her hands on her shorts and pulled out the journal. She smiled slightly and asked, "Ready?"

June 1, 1931

O. C. made it all happen. He souped up my outboard motor. It was fast. Last night just when nightfall came I took off to Canada. I went by myself. Probably because I didn't know what I was doing, but most of all I didn't want the weight of O.C. in the boat. I could carry more liquor that way without sinking. O.C. told his dad and he gave me the money to buy the Canadian whiskey.

Summer was coming and some tourist wouldn't mind the rot gut moonshine, but after one drink, they usually wanted some good stuff. Plus O.C.'s dad was thinking about expanding the back of his store to accommodate more people. People now call his drinking place, "The Blind Pig" and if it was a bit nicer, it would draw in more drinkers. O.C's dad thought I would do okay if I took the small boat and made my way over there at night. He made the connections for the liquor to be at the shore. I know the lake by heart. I fished it all my life and can navigate around the rocks without a light. I played it safe and only bought three cases. Placed them on the bottom of my boat and then I cut my motor and rowed back across the lake.

Old timers would say that there was a dry moon. That's a moon that is just a sliver and if you could tip it on its side, it wouldn't hold a drop of liquor. Dry moon or not, I didn't get caught. The stars covered the sky from horizon line to horizon line. My heart was pounding inside my chest and my mouth was dry with fear the whole time. It was exciting and I probably could've used a drink to give me some false courage, but I didn't want to pay for a bottle out of my earnings. When O.C.'s dad gave me my cut, my heart nearly gave out. I thought I was going to pass out. I have never seen so much money at one time. Fifty dollars for one night's work! That type of money will fill the cupboards and get some new clothes for my mom and little sisters. It's worth the risk, and I'm going to do it again.

"He's going to get caught," Arla said.

"I think they're starving. Barely living, no jobs and nowhere to go for help," I said. "This is not an easy place to make a living. It was a lot of money. Arla have you found out who wrote it yet?"

She shook her head, snapped the book shut. She handed it to me. "No and it's your turn to hold the book. That's as far as I read." She started to haul the gear back down to her boat. "I've got to get back to Gammy." She looked me straight in the eye and mockingly said, "Can you take care of Dylan and get him home okay?"

I'm trying to think of a snappy reply, but Dylan jumped in, "Arla, you need Henry to find your boat?" She was ready to burst out laughing. Her long dark hair was pulled back swirling across her back and those cornflower blue eyes were bright.

"Hey," I shouted out. "I can get both your sorry butts home. Arla, you would let me drive your boat?"

She bobbed her head, "Sure would. Dylan is still trying to figure out how to keep that monster he calls a motor running." I could see Dylan trying to think of some other insult to tease her. It was a perfect day. The sun was hot, the fishing great and I was with Dylan and Arla.

She gave Dylan a push barely hard enough to make him stumble. He howled and faked a staggering fall. Dylan falling was meant to get her stupid mad. He roared in mock pain as he hit the ground. However, Arla didn't know that pushing Dylan would save his life. All we heard was the sharp crack of a rifle as it pierced the perfect summer day.

Seven

WE KNEW A RIFLE SHOT WHEN WE HEARD IT. All three of us froze until Arla pulled me down next to the boats. "Dylan, are you okay?" She wildly called out while searching the area for the shooter. Dylan was crawling his way towards us.

I heard an eagle scream, "There." I pointed in the direction of Bushyhead Island. A boat started and sped away. It was too far to determine the make of the boat except that it was mostly white. Dylan was wheezing as I scrambled over to him. "Did you get hit?"

"No, but I swear I heard the bullet whiz by my head." Sweat wetted his brow. His face was a pasty gray. I thought he was about to pass out.

Reaching into the boat for a water bottle I encouraged him to drink. "You would've ruined a perfect day if you had been shot," I said.

He had a wild eye look of fear as he pulled hard on the bottle, half emptying it. A little bit of color flushed back into his face so I told him to take another drink. "Then again, I could drive the boat back home."

Dylan choked a bit on the water and smiled slightly, "Only if I'm dead are you going to drive my boat." I shivered a bit at how close that demand had come.

"Hey, you can put that on your list. Teach Henry to drive a boat," I joked.

Arla peered over the side of the boat. The lake looked clear. No boats with gun-toting crazies were around. She timidly stood up. For a good minute she stood still searching the lake, ready to dive down behind the boat. Dylan finally regained his normal color. She walked over to the nearby clumps of birch and pines. "I found the bullet." She sighted the direction of the shot, "Looks like it came from the direction of that boat." Arm stretched long, she pointed in the direction of Bushyhead Island. "Dylan, you could've been killed. Good thing I set you on your butt."

"For the record, you couldn't push me down if I didn't want to go down. But, this time, thanks for the push. I just don't understand why anyone would want to take a pot shot at us." Dylan stood and steadied himself by brushing the dirt off him. "If they meant to scare us, it worked. I was scared."

"They could've killed us. I think we should tell Uncle Mike someone's using us for target practice," I said and walked to the tree Arla was still examining. The bark of the pine tree had shattered where the bullet had penetrated into the wood. Pulling out my pocketknife, I pried fragments of bullet out. Showing them to Arla, I called Dylan over, "Look at this, it's a frangible bullet, meant for rats and chipmunks. It falls apart into pieces as soon as it hits something. Whoever shot this at us meant to hurt us."

Dylan walked over on shaky legs to look at the fragments. "Where did you learn that?"

"Science camp," I tried to say without gloating and got a small chuckle out of Dylan.

Arla gave me a smile. "Okay, science boy, I really need to get back to the store. The jerk that did this is long gone. How about I come over early tomorrow?" Her words were strong, but she nervously put the rest of her gear into the boat. The anchor hauled in, she got ready to push off.

Dylan shoved the bullet fragments into his pocket and hurried to his boat. "We'll follow you in, Arla. I want to fish off your point anyway."

"You don't have to. I'm sure they're gone," she said, but scanned the area again.

"I know, but I still want to fish the point, so if you see us following you, just ignore us. Get in, and I'll shove you off," Dylan insisted. He gave her a good shove. Her boat glided into deeper water. I finished putting all our gear in the boat and strapped on my lifejacket. Dylan was already fussing with the motor. I gave a push and jumped in. Both motors came to life, and Arla turned towards home with Dylan close behind. Three sets of eyes searched the area, but Arla was right, the shooter had disappeared.

It took at least twenty minutes before Arla landed her boat at the store's dock. She waved goodbye as Dylan turned his boat towards the point. "Are we really fishing the point?" I shouted over the motor.

"Nope, we're going to tell Dad that some nut's out on the lake trying to kill us."

The trip back was grim. I didn't want to think how close that bullet had come to Dylan. By the time we landed the boat at the cabin, it was late afternoon. Uncle Mike would be coming home soon, but as we walked into the cabin we saw the note. We were to fix dinner for ourselves and to stay off the lake. Dylan read the note again and immediately went to the gun safe to check on the contents.

"It's serious, whatever it is. We'll have to wait till he gets home. He took his gun. He never does that unless he patrolling. We might not be the only ones that got shot at today, probably just a random drunk shooting off rounds. Dad'll have to round him up before he does some real damage."

"Dylan, the chances someone's just randomly shooting and gets a shot off that close to us are phenomenal." I can't think of another reason except that the shooter was aiming for us. He either deliberately missed or he was a bad shot.

"You're not going to do one of your calculations on the probability of that occurrence are you?" mocked Dylan.

"No, but something isn't adding up. I don't think someone was squirrel hunting in the middle of the lake. If someone's out there trying to scare us, they're doing a good job, and if they're trying to kill us, why?" Stomping back to the kitchen, I wanted something to eat. I was uneasy, something felt missing. Why would anyone want to shoot Dylan? There were pieces of the puzzle missing, and I couldn't figure them out.

Supper was going to be sandwiches since we had no fish left. I was piling the turkey and cheese on bread when a thought occurred to me. "That guy we saw over at Little American. He was carrying a gun."

Dylan was about to chomp down on his sandwich but stopped midair. "Yeah, I've been thinking about that. It could've been a crazy tourist. We get some real wackos up here. They think they need to protect themselves from wolves or bears or something and feel compelled to carry a gun. They don't realize that, most the time, bears and wolves stay clear of people."

It was true. All the times I had been up here, we just didn't see bears or wolves that often. We had to go look for them or have a chance sighting. "He had that pickaxe. He was out to find gold."

"That's granite bedrock. A pickaxe won't touch it," said Dylan.

"So he's stupid or just doesn't know any better," I said while plowing through a sandwich.

"For sure, he wasn't from around here. Locals know that rock's granite," Dylan replied. "They'd just use dynamite."

I sniggered. It was the local joke that Grandpa Wilder had gotten sick of the shallow channel in front of the cabin. Being stubborn as a mule, he placed several sticks of dynamite in the channel. Of course he used way too much. The explosion was heard all the way across the lake. He did get the channel deeper. He also threw enough mud and rock to coat the cabin. Grandma was so livid that she made him scrub it all off before she would let him enter the cabin. It took two days.

We finished our sandwiches when Dylan asked, "You have the journal, right?"

"No, Arla still has it." I had completely forgotten about it after the shot.

Dylan gave me a sly look, "I've got a craving for ice cream. Some really good homemade ice cream. Let's head over to see Arla and check out if her freezer is still working."

We left a note for Uncle Mike and biked over to the store. We walked into the store that smelled of a combination of leeches, minnows, and ice cream. In a strange way, it was comforting. Arla was behind the cash register with a stack of papers, flipping through them one by one.

"Hey," I said, "did the freezer survive?"

"It's limping by, still working, but I'm suspicious it'll die any moment." She stood and stretched. I took a good look around. The store was empty.

"Business is good, I see," I said and walked over to the freezer that hummed and pinged.

"It's a bit slow tonight. I'm glad. It's just me. Gammy wants to finish reading her book. I was just going over some bills." The paper pile was at least two inches thick.

"That's a pretty big stack, Arla," I said as Dylan peered into the freezer top.

"It takes money to make money," is all she said. Rolling up her sleeves she grabbed an ice cream scoop. "We have chocolate and strawberry. What do you want?"

"Yes," Dylan and I both replied.

"Should have known. Bowls?"

"Yes," again we replied. Arla already had two ceramic ice cream bowls in her hand. Not those small little paper cups so many ice cream shops have, but heavy cream-colored bowls. She piled the bowls high with alternating scoops of chocolate and strawberry.

We pulled up stools to the checkout counter and dove in. The rich creamy flavor of chocolate and fresh strawberries flooded my mouth. "Arla you could sell this recipe and make a zillion bucks."

"No, I can't," she uttered. She was back concentrating on the bills. "Gammy would skin me alive if I gave out the recipe." Finally, she pulled out one bill and proclaimed, "And we have a winner. Peterson's Dairy gets paid this week." She slipped out a slim checkbook from under the counter and filled out a check. We were halfway through the ice cream by the time she had made out the envelope and placed it in the out box for mail. I had seen her make out checks before but it still amazed me.

Suddenly, I've got a serious brain freeze going on. The ice cream headache burns from my roof of my mouth to the top of my head. I waited a moment to let my brain thaw. The ache disappeared. Arla pulled out the journal.

She opened the book and Dylan stretched out his legs. I shoved in another mouthful.

June 10, 1931

Things were going so well. I should've known that it would get bad. I made three more runs and had no trouble at all. I can move five cases of Canadian whisky over at a time. For the first time ever, I have money in my pocket. The tourists are coming in for the summer and O.C.'s dad wants me to go over as often as I can. That wasn't the problem.

I've had no trouble on my midnight runs, but business got too good and it's drawing the wrong type of attention. O.C.'s dad already bought off the local police. Guess they like their liquor. They come in after shift and drink on the house. The feds are too busy chasing the bootleggers down. They want to cut the flow to Chicago and really don't care about us. This is bigger trouble.

Some of Capone's thugs came into O.C.'s shop yesterday and said that moonshine was okay but too much of the prime stuff was being wasted up here. The threat came with a baseball bat. They smashed up the store a bit along with a warning. Give them the good stuff or else. They took all the Canadian whisky that O.C.'s dad had on hand and then beat him up. He limps bad and has two black eyes and a nose that looks twice its size. It has to be broken. He wants me to go on another run tonight, but what if Capone's goons come after me?

I told O.C.'s dad that I couldn't and he understood, but I lied. I have enough money now to start my own run, buy the whiskey on my own and then sell it to the highest bidder. I'll stash the whiskey till things cool down and then sell it. Nobody will find my hidey hole. I leave tonight at midnight for my first run.

"Who is this guy?" my spoon rattled around in the empty bowl. I grabbed Dylan's empty bowl and slipped behind the counter to rinse them out.

Arla studied the front inside cover and then flipped to the back inside cover. "There's nothing here. Unless he's going to identify himself, we may never know."

"Look, we know he or someone stashed the book in the rafters of the cabin. It was built in the early 1930s. Maybe he was the first owner," Dylan said.

"He was too poor to own a house. But he might've worked on the house." Arla closed the journal and tucked it back down under the counter. "He never made mention of working as a carpenter, but he did write about finishing eighth grade. He wanted to go to high school, but couldn't. He was supporting his mom and sisters." She got up to wash the ice cream bowls when Uncle Mike walked into the store.

Uncle Mike was in the green gear of the U.S. Customs and Border Patrol along with a full day of dirt and grime. A cautious smile creased his tired face. He gave Dylan a soft slap on the back and nodded to Arla and me. "Good to see you guys. First, thanks for the note and second, did you eat all the ice cream?"

Arla was already reaching for the scoop. "Chocolate or strawberry?"

"Yes," he said and added. "Can you pack a quart to go? I want to get some of this grime off before I eat anything."

"Tough day, Uncle Mike?" I noticed how weary he looked. Deep lines of stress etched his face. His shoulders sagged with fatigue. Dried muck of a muskeg bog coated his boats and his pistol still hung from his side.

"You could say that, Henry. Arla, I need to talk to Gammy. Is she around?"

"She's really tired. I think she went to bed. I can get her if you want." Arla pushed on the top on the quart of ice cream and sat it just inside the freezer to keep cold.

Uncle Mike began to say it would wait, but then hesitated, "Arla, you'll hear of this sooner or later." He paused to blow out a breath. "There's been a murder on Rainy."

Eight

W HO?" DYLAN EXCLAIMED, but Arla and I were looking at each other wondering about our shooter.

"We're working on that. No one I know, so we're running his prints to get an ID." Uncle Mike sank down on a stool.

"Where was he found?" I asked, hoping it was not in the vicinity of Arla's island.

"On Bushyhead."

My stomach got that hollow sick feeling. Bushyhead was in eyesight of Arla's island. "He was found in the old gold mine," Uncle Mike added.

Arla turned pale as straw "How," she stammered. "How did he die?"

"Gunshot to the chest, as far as we know. The body will be sent to the coroner for examination. He'll take a good look. The victim was gunned down this morning."

"What?" all three of us said at the same time.

"He was probably shot early morning," Uncle Mike said suspiciously. "Why?"

We started talking all at once, tales of gold hunting, shore lunch, the shooting and the pseudo park ranger in a canoe. He calmly listened to all us jabber until we all paused to take in a breath. Ordering up some more ice cream for all of us, he pulled off his hat and took out a tablet. We sat in a circle around him. When we all had ice cream in our mouths, he explained that he wanted to hear each of our stories one by one. He pointed to Dylan to start and by twenty minutes we were done.

"Arla, can I go out to the island to look at your camp site in the morning?" Uncle Mike snapped the tablet shut. "I want to look at that bullet strike."

"Sure, do you need me to go with you?" Arla was stacking empty ice cream bowls.

"No, I'm good. You only have that one camp site?"

Arla nodded as she washed the bowls, "It's the only site I use, there might be a few other spots, but Gammy and I always use the beach.

Dylan stood up and pulled the bullet fragments out of his pocket. "Henry thought it was a frangible bullet."

Uncle Mike took the handful of fragments and took a close look before he poured them into a plastic evidence bag. "Good call, Henry. I think you might be right. But here's the bad news." He tucked the bag into his jacket pocket. "I want you all to stay off the lake, especially around Arla's island and Bushyhead. At least for a while. You can fish in our bay."

Dylan groaned so loud I thought Uncle Mike would say something, instead he gave him a sympathetic look, "I know it stinks, but until we find the person who did this or we believe he's gone, that's the rule."

"Arla, you and Gammy are out here all by yourselves. I'm going to have someone swing by here in the evening to check up on you."

"We're fine. I can close up a bit earlier. We're not getting that much business late at night anyway, and the gas pumps are still open around the clock. I'll close before sunset."

"Just make sure you're locked up tight every night and don't open the door to anyone you don't know. Does your marine radio still works?"

Arla chuckled, "Oh, yeah. Gammy loves that thing. If I'm a minute late while out on the lake she gets that thing crackling and tells me off."

"Good, you can call us on the emergency channel if you need us. I'll take that quart of ice cream. Guys, throw your bikes in the back of the pickup." Uncle Mike stood up and took a good look around the store. "I'm going to do a walk around the outside of the store, and then I'll let you close up." He dusted his hat off before putting it back on. "You okay with all of this, Arla?"

Arla tossed her hair back and shrugged, "We don't keep much cash on hand We lock up every night. I'll check the doors before I go to bed."

"Good," he said.

By the time our bikes were in the back of the truck Uncle Mike walked the perimeter of the store. He smiled an approval when he saw we didn't forget the ice cream.

"Looks locked up tight. Gammy isn't dumb. She has some serious locks on the doors and windows." The truck rolled out of the parking lot. Instead of heading back to the cabin, Uncle Mike turned on the road heading for the boat landing.

The state boat landing had been remodeled two years ago and now sported a concrete ramp and new dock. The wide sloping concrete ramp leading into the water made unloading boats from trailers easy. The nearby lot was full of trucks and empty trailers. We cruised into the lot. Uncle Mike slowly drove looking over the trucks. "All locals," he said more to me than Dylan.

That's the advantage of living in a small town. Uncle Mike knew just about everyone. I saw a sea of trucks and trailers while Uncle Mike knew all the owners. The ice cream was starting to melt in my lap when Uncle Mike cut the engine and reached for his hat. I put the ice cream down on the floor.

Opening the door, he said, "Stay here." Dylan and I sat in the dark and watched him walk towards the shore. A boat was coming in. Coasting up to the dock, Uncle Mike caught the tossed rope. As soon as the boat touched the dock, a man as burly as Uncle Mike jumped out. I heard Dylan suck in his breath.

"That's one of the Helgason brothers. Both of them dropped out of school by tenth grade. They're trouble. Dad knows them well," Dylan whispered.

The evening was cool and still. Some loons were calling to each other across the lake with the frogs sending a few croaks out from the nearby marsh. Otherwise the night was quiet, ready to carry our words over the landing. I leaned closer to Dylan.

"What has Uncle Mike caught them doing?" I whispered back. The other Helgason brother jumped out, and together they towered over Uncle Mike. They had a stringer of fish and Uncle Mike was taking a look at the catch. They stood a bit too close to him, but Uncle Mike didn't step away.

"Pretty much breaking the fishing law about fish size. It's either too many or too big. Dad swears dead fish follow them. They see Dad, and they start throwing the big ones back in the lake. They always claim that the dead fish aren't theirs."

"They also like to go back and forth across the lake to Canada without reporting in." Dylan pointed to a small blue shed off the side of the boat landing. It's a call station where you phone in when you returned from Canada. There're enough planes in the sky and cameras to know when you cross and don't report back in.

Uncle Mike tipped his hat and turned back to the truck. Getting in, he turned the engine on and sighed louder than the engine. "Those two give me job security. However, for once, they have the right size and number of walleye. Of course, I don't think they would've told me a thing even if they saw anything suspicious out on the lake."

We watched one of the brothers back his truck and trailer down the ramp to load their boat. Uncle Mike placed his hat back on the dashboard and wove around the trucks, his wheels crunching gravel.

We stored the ice cream in the freezer. I was about to head for bed when Dylan signaled for me to follow him into his bedroom. It was a small cabin bedroom with a bed made from small pine logs and dresser built into the wall. We sat cross-legged on the bed. Dylan pulled out a pack of cards and shuffled them, "Five card draw, okay?"

I nodded and the cards started flying my way. I arranged the five cards in my hand and silently groaned. If it wasn't the worst hand in history, it was the worst that I'd ever held. I wanted to toss the whole hand when I noticed that Dylan had set his hand down.

"You know we didn't tell Dad about the journal."

I palmed my cards and said, "Easy to forget with getting shot at and someone being murder. Kinda trumps a diary."

"More than likely Arla will bring the book tomorrow and I think we need to finish reading the thing."

"Okay, but don't you think we have other problems on our hands. Like who is our shooter and did he kill the guy?"

Dylan's eyebrow always twitched when he thought hard and right now it was twitching in a quick beat. "Who would want to kill us? It doesn't make any sense. It's Arla's island. Everyone from around here knows that. It was a big deal when Arla's folks died. She was little, and Gammy had to get a court order to proclaim that she could inherit the island. Dad said that everyone knows how much her mom and dad loved that place. It was the right thing to give it to her. It's not like Rainy Lake has a shortage of islands."

Card playing was done for the night, so I threw my cards to him. He must had agreed because he stashed the pack away and leaned back against his pillow. "Does Uncle Mike have any enemies?" I asked.

"Maybe. Dad has put away plenty of crooks, but that's the government law enforcement office and not just him. I think he's liked enough by everyone."

"Besides terrorists crossing the border from Canada, what else does he look out for?"

"Not alcohol so much, but drugs cross over and crooks like to escape to Canada so they are always trying to sneak across. But Dad claims that they're never too imaginative or they think the Border Patrol are stupid. They're pretty easily caught."

My head was spinning from thinking or from too much ice cream either way Dylan wasn't coming up with any new ideas either. I was ready for bed. I started to leave when I said, "We're going to solve the journal mystery tomorrow. I hope Gammy will feel okay to watch the store tomorrow."

"Gammy's tough. Arla will be here," Dylan called out as he turned off his light.

Nine

THE HAMMOCK WAS STRUNG between two poplar trees that stood guard over the lake. Arla had a leg hung over the side. It was her big toe that was doing all the work. Pushing herself back and forth, she watched us finish the yard work. The sun seemed brutal this morning as I hurried to finish the lawn. The journal sat in her lap. We had all agreed to finish the book.

Uncle Mike had left early in the morning for Arla's island but also posted a list of chores on the fridge. Dylan and I crashed down on the grass besides her. Two dripping cold glasses of water were held over the top of us. Arla had felt pity on us. Minnesota summers were mild. A hot day on Rainy would be in the eighties, but the sun didn't have to cut through all the city grime and pollutants. It was a clean sun, and it was hot. The water tasted wonderful as it slid down my throat. I chugged the whole glass and noticed that Dylan did the same thing. We set our glasses down and waited for Arla.

She nodded, pushed her big toe to set the hammock in motion and began.

June 20, 1931

I'm going to be rich man. I have cases of fine Cana-
dian whisky in my hiding spot. No one will find it. I had
a scare the other night when I thought I saw a flash of
light ahead of me on my way back across the lake. Who-
ever it was never saw me. I changed direction and went
behind Major Robert's Island and hid in the sand bay for
an hour. Then I made my way to my hiding hole. O.C.
was already there to help me unload the cases.

I'm giving him a cut for his help. His dad bought some
whiskey from me, but just enough to keep his customers
coming. He has to make a living and even Capone can't
scare him enough to close up the shop. The money is just
too good, besides Capone is too busy with the gang war
going on in Chicago with Baby Face Nelson. O.C. is wor-
ried that Capone won't take kindly to his dad selling good
whiskey again. I tell O.C. that we'll offer to sell only to
him if he will overlook his dad selling good liquor. I think
it's a good plan.

The boat is unloaded and we're heading back home
just as the sky was turning from black to blue gray. It's a
new morning and I'm sure this deal will make money.

Arla paused, "So this kid thinks he can swing the deal
with a Chicago mobster? I think he's being pretty stupid."

"He's been clever enough to avoid getting caught by
the feds. Maybe Capone wants to deal. He has to get the
liquor somewhere. Plus Capone wants it before Baby Face
Nelson gets it."

My back was cushioned by grass as I looked up into the sky with floating clouds.

Dylan was on his belly propped up on elbows, "He doesn't take into account the danger of it all. He's like us. One minute we're sitting around stuffing our faces with fresh walleye and the next we're in the dirt with a bullet singing over our heads. It just didn't seem real yesterday."

"Felt real to me," Arla said testily. "It's not like we were asking to get shot at. We're on my island minding our own business."

"Okay, I think we can all agree that yesterday really happened. Let's see if we can figure out where's his hiding spot. Read on Arla." I gave a look to Dylan to shut up and let her read as she started again.

July 1, 1931

Now I know how evil people can be. O.C. and I are hiding trying to figure out a plan. Last night Capone's men went to O.C.'s place and started in on the old caged bear, teasing and poking him with their rifles. His dad pleaded for them not to let him go. He's too old to find his own food and would die, but they didn't care. The three of them let the bear out. They yelled and hollered at him to get. They shouted that it was better to be free and dead than dying in a cage. That old bear just walked two steps out of the cage and sat down and stared at them. They laughed as they shot him.

They walked over to the famed pig and bragged how they wanted bacon for the morning. One of them asked

O.C.'s dad if a blind pig tasted any different. O.C.'s dad said nothing as he watched them shoot his pig. They laughed and said that the place could now be called the "Dead Pig" instead of the "Blind Pig." At that point O.C.'s dad told him that nothing good was going to come out of this. He had to run at the first opportunity and take his baby sister and hide. O.C. said he was so scared that he didn't think his legs could move.

O.C. was ready to bolt when Capone's thugs aimed their guns at them. O.C.'s dad shouted out to wait. He claimed he had a couple of cases of whiskey hidden in the store. O.C. knew that was lie. I was going on another run tonight because he claimed it was all gone. O.C.'s dad was pressuring me to sell him a few more bottles and I was going to, but not now. The thugs looked at each other for a moment and then seem to come to a silent agreement. At the nod of their heads, O.C.'s dad led them into "The Blind Pig" and O.C. knew that this was the moment. He turned and ran.

He picked up his baby sister and the Indian woman and went to my house. Tears were running down his face when he banged on the door. My mom took one look at him with his sister in his arms and guessed that things were bad. She ushered them in and immediately O.C. asked if I would go back with him to rescue his dad. I wished I had said no.

Ten

Arla stopped and snapped the journal shut. She stared out over the lake at the edge of the bay. The steady hum of a boat reached us. Uncle Mike was in a patrol boat coming around the point. Dylan got up and walked down to the dock. "Arla, maybe Dad found something at the island," he called over his shoulder.

We're all down at the dock as the large boat approached. Dylan reached for a landing rope, but Uncle Mike shook him off.

"Arla, just to let you know that we found nothing else out on your island, except for the bullet strike in the tree. We took a quick spin around, but you really don't have any good landing spots except that sand beach."

"Thanks, Mr. Wilder. I'm sure it was just some crazy person taking pot shots," she replied.

"It's hard to figure out the why. Guys, I have to get back to work. I'll see you later tonight. Don't wait supper on me." The boat backed away from the dock and turned towards Bushyhead.

"One guess, where he's headed today," I uttered as we made our way back to the hammock.

"We just don't get murder around here. We get shooting accidents, but a murder is rare." Dylan plopped back down on the grass and got a smirk on his face. "You want me to read, Arla? You tired out?"

"You can walk, talk *and* read? The list of your achievements is ever growing," she teased. Dylan glared and threw a partially melted ice cube at her. She dodged it easily and beamed, "Thanks for the ice, but I'm good." She raised her glass at him. "And I've gotten use to his writing. Okay, so he just wrote that he was sorry he went to rescue O.C.'s dad." Arla got back into the hammock swinging and opened the journal.

I smelled it first, that heavy acid scent of burning oil and metal. We're running through the woods taking a short cut to the store. The fire was so large that we could see the flames over the tops of the trees. O.C. groaned and started to run faster, orange flashes of color blinked around tree trunks as we got closer. We came out of the trees and saw nothing but flames and smoke. The heat of the fire kept us back. O.C. wanted to burst into the flaming store, but I held him back. There was no hope of his dad surviving if he was still in there and we both knew he was. O.C. dropped right to his knees and cried.

It was my good sense that told me to get the heck out of there. I was searching around us hoping that we weren't sitting ducks in the water for Capone's thugs. It took all my strength to pull O.C. away and tell him my plan.

We had to disappear. Mom and the girls had to leave before Capone found out where they were. I couldn't risk their lives. So I made O.C. get up, and we went back to the house. I told Mom to pack up and go visit her sister down in Duluth. I gave her all my money, so they could take the Greyhound bus along with O.C.'s sister and the Indian lady. She somehow knew that O.C.'s dad was gone, but she didn't say a word. She didn't even question where all the money came from. She just slipped it into her pocket and went about her business of packing. I kissed her good-bye and O.C. and I made our escape.

July 5, 1931

O.C. and I have been hiding here for days. I was out exploring because I was bored, but I hurried back. We're isolated here yet I had that feeling that someone was watching me. The hair on the back of my neck rose up and I got that cold shudder that made me think I wasn't alone. I looked hard but saw nothing through the big pines. I told O.C. I had a bad feeling. He too thought someone was watching. I told him it was probably a killer chipmunk and made us laugh, but I'm getting spooked.

We've made good use of our time here. The place I keep all the cases of whisky was just a big cave. So O.C. and I shored up the entrance way with wood, and we carved our initials into one of the supports.

O.C. thinks we should open our own "blind pig." It is pretty enough here. The water laps almost to the cave entrance and walls are layers of pink and gray granite. We could sell the liquor right out of this place, but I don't think so. This was my dad's secret spot. I keep hoping he might show up some day. I want this place to be kept a secret.

I'm going into town tonight to sell the whiskey. I won't sell to Capone—it is too dangerous. I made arrangements with Baby Face Nelson's men the other night and if I can, I will sell all that I have and get out of this business. It's not worth our lives. We're going to meet at Hell's Point. It's not far and sits at the entrance of Put-in Bay. The lake can be unforgiving there when the Canadian wind blows up waves five and six feet high. A new cabin is halfway built on the point. For now it's deserted and I can get in and out quick by boat. Once all is sold I will go and get Mom and the girls and maybe we can start a new life else-where far from here.

Arla closed the book and ran a hand over the aged cover. "That's the end of the journal. There's no mention of who he is." She stood and stretched, the hammock swung to a stop.

My mind was racing with scenarios. "It's here where he met the buyers. Our cabin was the one he was talking about." I got a chill that slid down my back.

Dylan pointed to the nearby shore that jutted into the lake. "That's Hell's Point. He must've stashed the journal in the rafters that night. But, why?"

"He was in danger," Arla quietly said. "Deep down I think he knew something bad would happen. He must have been scared out of his mind."

We all got up and stared at the cabin wondering what happened that night. It was a risky game they played.

Arla started to walk towards the cabin. She called over her shoulder, "Anyone hungry besides me?" It was long past lunch. We followed her like cattle.

"I think he got killed. Dylan, you said it yourself that murder is rare around here, but Capone had no trouble with killing," I said. My legs were taking long strides to keep up with Dylan. He was power walking to the cabin. Dylan loved the lunch idea.

"I bet he ran right through this cabin, looking for a spot to hide his book," I quietly said. The cabin door creaked open like it always did. I wondered if it creaked that night so many years ago.

"It's creepy. I hope he didn't die," Arla said. She wrapped her arms around herself.

Dylan muttered, "He probably made a load of money, picked up his mom and little sister and took off for California. Where he made a fortune selling fried walleye sandwiches and lived happily ever after." The cabin felt cool after sitting out in the sun. The hair on the back of my neck stood up as I thought of a scared kid looking for a place to hide his book.

Dylan examined the empty fridge before he sighed and closed the door. He started on one side of the kitchen searching cabinets for anything edible.

Arla sat down at the kitchen table, "I don't think there were many 'happier ever after' stories back then. It's really hard to break away from your home town. I bet it was harder back then." She pushed her dark hair back and gazed out the window.

I wondered if she's speaking for herself. She has had nothing but responsibility since she was tall enough to stand behind the store counter. "Arla, do you want to ever get away from here? Like travel or go to school or just go someplace that's warm in the winter?" I couldn't help but think that in many ways she was trapped. Gammy was legally her guardian, but Arla was tied to the store. I felt bad. I had never asked if she had traveled out of northern Minnesota. I wondered if she had even been to Minneapolis. Gammy needed help. Arla was anchored to the place.

"I think about it," she stated, "but when I check my billion dollar trust fund, I just don't want to bother with that pesky paper work to get the money and do all that tedious traveling." She said it like a joke, but there was something sad about the way she spoke.

"Besides, Gammy doesn't want to travel. She needs me now and I have to be someplace. Here's better than the other choices even if I have to put up with Dylan. Someone has to help him get through school." She sent a lopsided grin to Dylan and got a grunt back.

Dylan opened the fridge again as though something magically appeared since he looked five seconds ago. "O.C. and friend ran away, became pirates, and made a fortune."

"Sounds good to me," I said and watched Dylan. He was on a serious food hunt.

"Right, I don't think they had the pirate option. I think he was killed. He saw the danger and hid the journal, hoping someone would find it and know he was here," Arla said and gave Dylan an exasperated look. She got up to join the food hunt. She walked to a tall cabinet opening the doors wide. It was sparse, just a few packages of dried beans and almost empty jar of peanut butter.

Standing on her tiptoes she felt with a hand on the top shelf for anything that could be eaten. Groaning with effort she pulled on a stack of papers. Several packages of Japanese noodles fell out along with some newspapers. "Hey, we can make some soup," she said picking up the noodles and the newspapers.

I took a closer look. The papers were brittle and yellow. The newsprint faded with age. "These are the newspapers that Uncle Mike found in the wall." I carefully placed them on the table and saw that it was *The International Falls Daily Journal*. Pointing a finger at the date, the front page was a big picture of burned rubble. I read, "July 2, 1931. This is about the fire. I bet our guy is here." The paper gave a dry crackle as I unfolded it. My eyes were glued on the headline. "Three Missing in Jarvason's Fire." I read out loud.

Eleven

I DARTED AHEAD IN THE ARTICLE as Dylan and Arla held their breath. They leaned in close trying to find a name. I quickly began to read.

> On the evening of July 1, 1931, a fire broke out at Jarvason's on the outskirts of town. The local popular garage and dry goods store had been a landmark in the community for over ten years. Owner John Jarvason (39), his son, O.C. (14) and friend, Rory McDougal (13) are missing and presumed dead.

"Rory McDougal," I repeated. "That's our guy!"

"He disappeared that night along with O.C. We know they were hiding out for days." Arla opened the journal again and began to page through the writing, "What happened to you, guys?" she whispered.

I scanned the rest of the article. "The paper claims that Rory's mom last saw them together when they went to check on O.C.'s dad. She said she didn't know why except that O.C. was upset and had brought the Indian woman and his little sister." That confirmed what Rory wrote in the journal."

I carefully opened the paper looking for any other news. "Maybe she didn't go to Duluth to see her sister."

"She could've heard about the fire and stayed to find him," noted Dylan. "Or the bus didn't leave till late and the reporter found her before she left." He thumbed through the newspaper with me. "Is there a later paper?"

"No, this is it, and why was this paper stuck in the wall?" I carefully folded the paper back into its creased quarters. "Who put this paper in the wall and what connection did they have with Rory?"

"Something happened to them." Arla got up from the table to fill a pan with water and sat it on the stove to boil. "We may never find out. Someone killed them. Rory was making a lot of money transporting whiskey across the border. Capone didn't mind him running the risk to get the liquor. He was just greedy and wanted it all, that's why he threatened O.C.'s dad."

I got up from the table to get some bowls out. "Capone wasn't a nice guy. What if he heard that Rory was going to sell to Baby Face Nelson? He could've killed him as a warning to sell just to him."

Dylan was in the fridge again. He pulled out the last two eggs and bread. He opened the bread bag. There were only a few slices left. "The Dylan special?" he asked. We nodded our heads to agree. "He could've been killed by Capone's competitors or even by other runners across the lake that didn't want the competition or even captured by the law."

"I know. He became a pirate and lived happily-ever-after," Arla taunted Dylan.

"I don't think that happened," I said. I did the honor of putting the noodles in the boiling water and mentally counted off three minutes before pouring the spice packs into the mix. Dylan cracked the eggs into a bowl and scrambled them. He tossed them into the soup while Arla stirred quickly. The eggs instantly cooked and Dylan dumped hot sauce into the soup.

"I do have an idea, since we are limited to the bay area," I said and gave the ladle to Arla. She spooned the spicy egg soup into the bowls. "Why don't we find the hiding spot?"

The toaster popped. Dylan brought the toast over to the table. We sat down to eat. "Look," I said and made my case. "He gives clues throughout the journal. You guys really know the lake and maybe we can figure it out." I spooned up a bit and slurped it down. It was pretty good. "There might be more clues in the hiding spot."

"Why not," Dylan shrugged his shoulders. "We can fish the bay in an hour, two max."

"Because Rainy Lake has hundreds of islands on it?" Arla skeptically replied. "You're delusional if you think we can find the island."

"You're right," Dylan began with a wry look. "Henry and I can explore. You stay at the shop and knit or do something that girls do. Henry, what do you think girls like to do?"

I really didn't want to get Arla mad, but the words just spilled out, "Read vampire books?" She gave me a hurt look. I quickly added, "They can be good, especially if they have werewolves. There's nothing better than a good were-wolf vs. vampire fight with lots of blood."

Dylan tried not to snigger. He gave Arla a quick smile. "I don't understand why girls fall in love with blood-sucking guys that deprive them of their free will?" he said. "But then again, I'm delusional."

Arla's cornflower-blue eyes glowered at him. Her icy glare never left Dylan as she said, "Henry, make out a list of the clues. I've got to get back to Gammy and real work." Shoving the journal at me, she headed for the door. "I'll be back in the morning to figure it out." She called out just as the screen door slammed, "Dylan, be a good girl and wash the dishes."

I laughed, "She falls for that girl comment every time."

Twelve

LATER THAT NIGHT I SAT IN MY ROOM and made a list of all the hiding spot clues left in the journal. Rory had said he hid behind Major Robert's Island when he thought someone had spotted him. We could see Major Robert's Island from our dock. Another clue was about pines. Rory had felt isolated, so he was either deep in the woods or on an island. I wrote down, "Major Robert's Island, pine trees and isolation." Rory liked how the water came up to the entrance way so it had to be on the lakeshore or island. The cave was rock so probably granite. I wrote, "on the water and big cave." There was a comment about not being far from Hell's Point, so I wrote that down. I looked over the clues. This was really a stupid idea.

It could be anywhere. I slipped the list into the journal and went to bed. I tossed and turned for two hours thinking where his hiding hole might be and if it was worth the trouble to find it. I finally fell asleep dreaming of a cave filled with cases of whiskey. I woke up wondering if Rory made his sale before he disappeared.

As the sun started to light up my room, I got that creepy feeling that someone was watching me. My eyes popped open. Someone was looking through the window. I gasped. Then I realized I was being stupid. I was on the second floor. The eagle was peering in. He puffed himself up like he was ready to shriek, but instead he gave me a glaring look and took off. That was definitely not his routine. His flight forced me out of bed. Looking out the window, Uncle Mike was up and walking around.

His arrival home was after all my tossing and turning. Dressed for his work, he had his pistol strapped to his side, a sure indicator he was going to be out in the field for the day. A cup of steaming coffee was in his hand. He stared out over the lake watching the sun rise.

I pulled on a sweatshirt and went outside to greet him. For once, I was up before Dylan. The early morning wake-ups were starting to feel normal as I walked down to the shore.

"Hey, Uncle Mike." The guy looked exhausted and could probably use a pipeline of coffee directly into his veins. Usually he looks like he could run down any crook, but today he seemed wiped. "How's the investigation going?" I asked optimistically, hoping for a positive answer.

"We're chasing our tails," he said. "No leads yet and the killer just vanished." He came over and gave me one of his crushing shoulder hugs. "This isn't the way I wanted you to spend your summer, holed up in the bay. However, it'll give you a chance to learn to swim."

I gave a small groan. "Dylan and Arla are keeping me plenty busy." Gold hunting and the mystery solving around the disappearance of Rory and O.C. might keep us busy for the rest of the summer. I peered into the dark water depth off the dock. At this time of the morning the water looked calm, maybe even inviting. However, just the thought of jumping off the dock made my heart thump.

"Good, but work on the swimming. I'll try to get back at a normal time tonight and we can go for a swim."

"Great," I said with as much enthusiasm as cleaning my room. "Can't wait."

Uncle Mike laughed and slapped me hard enough on the back to leave a mark. "Let's make sure Dylan's up and then I have to head out. I'm afraid you still have to stick close to home. What are the plans?"

"You know, hang with Arla, fish and swimming 101."

"You can do it, Henry," he reassured me.

I stared back into the water. Suddenly, the water looked menacing, deep and cold. I wouldn't even put my toe into it. It shouldn't be too hard to distract Dylan enough to skip the swim lesson. I was already thinking of ways when Uncle Mike's walkie talkie crackled on.

I heard the rundown of the night's events. There were no new leads and still no positive I.D. on the victim. Uncle Mike replied that he was leaving right away. He gave me a nod and said, "Swimming at the dock at 8:00 p.m. okay?"

I gave an "oh boy can't wait" look that was one step away from a grimace. He grinned as he made his way to his truck.

I entered the cabin to see Dylan shoving cereal into his mouth. He nodded and mumbled "hi" and then without slowing down emptied the cereal bowl. He said, "I heard. Swimming tonight. We're going swimming today, Henry. There's a nice sand bay right across the way. We'll head over there this afternoon and jumpstart the swimming lessons. Remember if you look like you're making progress, Dad won't hound you as much."

I knew that. I liked water. It was my drink of choice. Just my arms and legs didn't want to swim. I'd bounced on my toes for summers. Maybe it was the thought of swimming in the lake. Fish peed in that water. However, I knew it wasn't that. It was my fear of sliding under the water and not being able to break my head above the surface. The thought was stuck in my head. I couldn't shake the idea of being trapped and never making it to the top. Why I didn't go to a swim camp during one of my camp-filled summers at home? Maybe I was a chicken at heart.

The morning went by pretty fast until we realized that Arla hadn't shown up. We're on our bikes and soon walked into the Last Stop. I saw a young guy, around twenty behind the counter, scooping up shiners for a customer. "Hey, Dylan, how's it going?" He shouted out as he twisted and tied the bag.

"Hey, Pete, this is my cousin."

"Hey," I said as the whole line of customers gave me the once over.

Pete smiled and nodded a hello as he handed over the shiners. Dylan was examining the bait fish in the last tank. "That's some pretty big bait. Henry has caught fish smaller." I peered into the tank and saw gray speckled fish longer than my hand. Dylan was right. They were super-sized.

"You need big bait to catch big fish, Dylan." Pete looked at me and winked. His hands free of bait reached out to shake my hand, "Great to meet ya, Henry. Arla says you're here for the summer?"

I said, "Yeah, until I start catching more fish than Dylan. Then he'll ship me back home." I returned the handshake.

Dylan groaned, "That's not gonna happen. I'll be stuck with you forever."

Pete was just short of six feet tall and looked like a body builder. He had no neck, and his faded t-shirt stretched around a chest of banded muscles. His hair looked brown but was clipped so short that his scalp showed through. He flashed a big grin that came easy. "Don't believe Dylan. You need big bait to get a trophy fish. A good twenty-pound pike would give you a good fight and a picture or two to brag to your friends back home." His firm handshake came with an intense eye contact and made my finger bones buckle. I'm grateful that he didn't crush my hand.

"I bet you're looking for Arla," he said. He tilted his head upstairs. "Gammy Mary had a tough morning. Arla's sitting with her. She called me in around 8:30 a.m."

"How sick is she?" Dylan asked.

"Don't know, but go on up. She mentioned that you might show up."

We headed for the door that hid the stairs. Normally locked, we entered the tight narrow stairway up to the second floor and knocked lightly on the door. Arla opened the door and placed a finger at her lips to hush us. We walked quietly in and sat at their small kitchen table.

I loved the small living quarters above the store that Arla called home. The living space had a kitchen tucked along one wall and two small bedrooms along the other wall. The furniture, walls and floors all had the warm patina of life. Every inch of spare wall space was tight with either books shoved onto shelves or pictures. On the wall were pictures of Arla's parents. Arm in arm with baby, Arla, squeezed tight between them. Arla was a copy of her mom. Lucy, while her dad, Ray, was tall and blond. The picture was taken on the island with them sitting on a large rock with a toddler-size Arla. There were pictures of Louie, Arla's grandfather, and Gammy together over forty years.

Young, middle age and old, some of the pictures were cracked and faded, some were yellowed black and white and some had the brown tone of early photographs. One faded black-and-white picture showed Louie and Gammy standing in front of the Last Stop and another with Lucy as a baby. There were many pictures of Lucy growing up in the store. A large wedding picture of Lucy and Ray was stuck in a bookcase. At the edge of the wall, was Gammy with Arla, who was barely able to see over the counter of the Last Stop. Picture frames of different colors and shapes were jammed on faded wallpapered walls surrounding a kitchen table for four, a comfy couch and broken in chintz chair.

We settled around the kitchen table, and Arla brought us milk, fresh baked chocolate-chip cookies and a rolled up map of Rainy Lake. I pulled the journal out of my backpack with pieces of paper sprouting from it. I had done my best to record all the references. I handed them to Dylan and Arla. "How's Gammy?" I softly whispered.

"She just caught a summer cold. It kept her up all night. If she could get some sleep, I think she'll be just fine." Arla glanced at the clock over the gas stove, "She's been sleeping for three hours and isn't coughing too bad. Pete was able to come in so I could sit with her." She unrolled the map of Rainy Lake. It stretched across the table. "What did you find?"

Dylan cut in and began in a soft teasing whisper, "Arla hired Pete because she has a crush on him."

"I hired Pete because he can count without using his toes and Gammy needs to take a break from time to time," Arla said glaring at Dylan.

"She thinks he's dreamy."

"I think you're stupid," she said and then turned to me. "Let's ignore him and hope he disappears. What did you find?"

I gave her the list and outlined the facts. "This isn't much, but I think we can make a guess." The lake stretched between the U.S. and Canada with the international border running down the middle of the lake. I pointed to the western side and at one of the narrowest parts of the lake. "The town of Ft. Francis, Canada is right across from International Falls, Minnesota, and that has not changed from the

1930s. The city is right across the Rainy River and not very far. It would serve as a place to get cases of whiskey and it has easy access by boat. Rory might have motored there, but he rowed the way back. If he simply went across the river to Ft. Francis, he would easily be caught, but he was not going to row across the entire lake, because he was limited by the number of hours in the night. Plus, he gave a clue that he never took off for Canada until after midnight."

All our attention was on the western part of the lake, trying to find a possible spot. Dylan said, "That means four hours of darkness, five tops at this time of year. It would be hard to row very far. Major Robert's Island is right here." Dylan points to thin strip of island that was close to the American shore. "It's a couple of miles from Ft. Frances."

"He hid there for a whole hour. His hideout couldn't have been too far away. He would have to race day light." Nose to the paper, I was examining the map in detail. "Look how close Hell's Point is to Major Robert's Island." My finger pivoted at the point that jutted out into the lake southwest of Major Robert's island. Our cabin sat right at that spot.

"How far do you think he can row in an hour?" Arla poised the question at me.

"Finally, I'm being appreciated for my brains," I said and Arla gave me a quick smile.

"Henry, you're always appreciated, especially how hard you work to take care of Dylan. It's a burden," she said.

"He's not too bad . . . for a cousin," I said and gave Dylan a one-sided smile. "Depending on the waves and wind and how much weight in the boat, I think he could make two or three miles an hour."

"I think we can assume that Rory wouldn't just go across the river to pick up the whiskey and then come right back. Too easy, and he would've been caught by the feds," Dylan said while trying to trace a pathway east from Ft. Francis that went to Major Robert's Island. "If he came this way, I don't think he would've made it much farther. The whiskey was heavy, and he had to unload it and get home while it was still dark."

Arla grabbed a pencil, "Let's use Major Robert's Island as a center point. If Rory rows for another hour that could mean another three miles from Major Robert's Island and includes this area." She marked the map with a sweeping arch that included shoreline and islands. "We'll use my island as an outer marker, and I think we should forget about the shore. Cabins were popping up all over during that time, and Rory would be too easily discovered."

"Islands it is," I said and started to count up the possibilities. I paused and asked, "Rory mentioned pine trees. Is it a clue?" In my mind, pine trees were everywhere up here.

Dylan answered, "He could have mentioned white, red or jack pines, maybe back then people would identify them by pines, tamaracks or cedars. It's odd. We have lots of trees."

"We can narrow it down. There're three islands. We can go explore them as soon as your dad gives the okay," Arla said as a noise came from a bedroom. Gammy appeared.

"No, you all didn't wake me. I've got enough sleep to shake this cold." She walked into the kitchen. She lit the stove burner under the pot of coffee.

"You look better. Sure you're okay?" Arla got up and gave her a hug.

"Now, scoot away," Gammy fussed. "I don't want you getting this bug." The water bubbled through the coffee pot while she examined the map. "Where are you trying to explore?"

"Gold," Dylan blurted out. "We're looking for gold. We figure there might be some more gold somewhere on Rainy Lake."

I looked at him and marveled at his quick thinking. I don't know why we wanted to keep Rory and O.C. a secret, maybe because it was ours to keep.

"There've been stories of gold strikes since the first find in the late 1800s. I heard them as a little girl." She slid into a chair at the table and pointed at Little American Island. "That discovery at Little American did nothing but break hearts and spirits. Rainy Lake City was born and died all in six years. My father was just a child when gold was discovered, but he remembered it well. Rainy Lake City was wild—more saloons than churches and more lying than telling the truth. If men weren't making up stories of the gold strikes, they were drinking at the saloon. In the end the gold didn't last and the town died." The coffee had perked long enough. She poured herself a cup and took a sip sighing as she swallowed.

"That was my great-grandfather?" Arla stopped her map gazing and asked, "I don't know much about him."

"Like so many men then, he died young. It was common to lose someone, either to the bitter winter or logging."

"How did he die?" Arla asked tenderly.

"I was young like you. He got kicked by a mule. The beast broke his leg. Some sort of blood poisoning or infection did him in. Lucky for me I found my Louie at an early age. We married young. It was his dream to run this store."

"Was it your dream, Gammy?" Arla asked.

"Of course. I was sixteen when we married. He was ten years older. He had saved up for years. It was an adventure and exciting for us. We worked hard and loved it." She patted Arla's hand. "Don't you be worrying I was unhappy here." She took another sip of coffee and looked about the room. "I love it here. It's my home and yours. But when I'm gone, Arla, this doesn't have to be your life. Sell the place, get an education. Travel the world. Don't let this place tie you down."

Tears appeared, and she gave Gammy another hug, "One, that's enough of that talk and two, this is my home. I love it here, even with the cranky freezer unit."

Gammy chuckled, "We should do something about that unit."

"Yeah, like throw it into the dumpster." Arla sat back down and laughed.

"So what stories." I was trying not to stare at the map. The three islands stared back at me. Two, I had never explored, but the third one I knew well.

Gammy started, "It's quite the story and has several versions, but the ending is all the same. My dad would tell it to us often."

"Tell us his version," I asked. My fingers silently tapped on the map on top of the islands.

Dylan finally brushed my fingers away to stop the tapping. Gammy continued, "I'm sure the story came with the finding of gold on Little American Island. Everyone wanted to get rich quick. Little American was not the only place they found gold. Big American, Bushyhead, Bad Vermillion, and close to Oveson's fish camp, all had some gold. Not much, but enough to fuel the stories of the big find. Everyone was looking for the vein that was so big they could pave the streets with gold. Of course, no one found it, and the streets were paved, but from all the rock rubble from the mines. No one ever found the big strike."

"Who started the rumor?" I asked. My attention finally focused on Gammy and away from wanting to find Rory's hide out.

"It's an old story. The Ojibwa have a tale of a golden river. They claim that it starts like a trickle and then floods the rock that it flows in. No fish swim in it nor do the loons call from it. It never freezes nor dries up, yet it sparkles with the sun. It's a river that stands still."

"How big was it?" Dylan probed.

"Back then, the old miners believed that it was huge, a mine that would take a lifetime to dig out. Just the hope of it would get my father talking about possible locations of the mine for hours."

"Nobody found it?" I asked.

"No, and everyone looked. Men and women spent their entire life looking for something that was probably nothing more but a foolish tale." Gammy took another sip of coffee.

Dylan pulled the map closer and started looking at the area around Little American. "Did the rumor ever include how big the mine was?"

"Oh, that was fun part of the story. The Ojibwa didn't have a way to measure weight, but the story claims that the mine was huge, the old miners thought at least a million."

We all stared at Gammy in silence, I finally sputtered, "A million dollars?"

"Oh, heavens no," she laughed, "a million ounces."

Thirteen

THAT'S 1.5 BILLION DOLLARS," I numbly said. I suddenly remembered the cartoon where some animated figure started chanting over and over again, "It's worth a million zillion gazillion dollars."

Arla snorted, "Sounds like something only a fool would go after. I'm just glad it's a billion dollars worth of gold, because that makes it more unbelievable." She's directed her words at Dylan.

"Henry, think of all that we could buy with a billion dollars. I'm going to buy a boat. At least twenty feet, fully loaded with a 200-horsepower motor."

"Yeah, sure, Dylan," Arla kidded. "You'll still have to wait three years before your dad would let you get a bigger boat."

Dylan completely ignored her. "Travel, too. I want to go everywhere and see everything. Henry, what would you buy?"

My mind was racing. Arla was right. We would never find the mine but it was fun to dream. "A car or even a boat. It's pretty cool up here. It'd be nice to have a place."

"Yeah, you could build one of those mansions with big screen TVs in every room and a computer command area and a heated indoor pool." Dylan's eyes were gleaming over the thought.

"That's the last thing that I would want. I think a log cabin would be great." I was thinking of one with a great view and basic. I chuckled out loud, "but indoor plumbing would be nice."

"How about you, Arla? What would you get first?" I asked.

"Reality checks for you guys," she sarcastically said. "You're dreamers. That story's been floating around for over a hundred years. I think someone would've found the 'River of Gold' by now. If it was real how come we don't have some big corporation here digging up the environment and looking for it?"

"You're probably right," I agreed, "but for a moment did you think the possibility was real? What popped in your mind? What would you get?"

Arla looked at Gammy, "Endless money? I think I would rebuild the Last Stop, or at least get a new freezer," she laughed.

"Don't you touch this place as long as I'm here, baby girl. However a new freezer would be nice," Gammy added. She stood up and stretched. "Now, I feel like a million bucks." She pointed a finger at Arla, "I know Pete is downstairs. So get out of here. Get me some more of those walleye."

Arla gave her a scrutinizing eye, "Are you sure?"

"Right as rain. Now get. I promise I'll rest and will only go down to relieve Pete for lunch." She made shooing motions with her hands. Arla's feet seem planted. I could tell she was not eager to leave. "I'm okay." Gammy gave her a push towards the door. "I'll be fine. Really. Go. I'm serious about those fillets."

Arla grabbed her jacket. We walked down the stairs. Pete was at the tanks scooping up black slimy leeches for a customer. "How's she doing?"

"I guess good enough to kick me out. Do you need help here?"

"Nope, it's steady but a good pace. I'm good. Going fishing?" he asked.

Dylan mumbled, "As much fishing as we can in the bay."

Arla opened a plastic bag and dipped a ladle full of shiners into a bag. "It'll be a challenge, but better than getting shot at."

Pete handed the leeches to a customer. "Wow! That's the talk of the lake. Murder on Rainy. A killer on the loose. Hope your dad gets them soon, Dylan."

"I'm sure he will," Arla jumped in. Dylan's frowned as Arla smiled and stepped closer. She stood too close and pushed her hair back behind one ear. "Do you mind staying for the afternoon?"

A smile broke across Pete's face that crinkled his eyes, "For you, not at all. Anytime you need me, you just have to give me a call."

"Thanks, Pete. I appreciate it."

Dylan gave a cough and grabbed the bag of shiners from her hand, "Let's go, Arla. We want to get those fish for Gammy." Arla slowly pulled back and then turned to give a small wave back at Pete. Her hair swirled out as she did a quick turn to leave.

We started to pedal our bikes back to the cabin when Dylan started in, "Oh, my, how nice that big strong Pete can help you out. 'Just call me if you need me?' Sounds like a greeting card." Dylan did some hard pedaling to kick up dirt. He called back over his shoulder to taunt her. "Oooh, I appreciate you sooo much."

We both slowed down to get out of the wake of dust. "If I didn't know my cousin so well, I would think he was jealous," I said.

Arla laughed, "Henry, he's like a brother to me. I've known him forever. He just wants a reason to give me a bad time."

"Maybe," I said. My cousin would be nuts not to notice how beautiful and funny, Arla was, even with all the kidding.

"Besides it's my job to give him a bad time," she said with a laugh. "Makes him appreciate girls."

By the time we rolled into the yard, Dylan was already loading up the boat. We made our way down to the dock just as he hopped into the boat. "Let's get going. The fish are waiting."

"Dylan, I don't think they're going very far in the bay." I reached down for a life jacket and snapped it on. Arla slid into the middle seat as I got in the front.

"There're no fish this time of year in the bay," he said as he backed the boat away from the dock. "You heard the orders. Gammy wants fish." He headed the boat out of the bay towards open water. "I think there's good fishing by Tuff Island," he shouted over the motor noise. I took a quick look around, expecting a gun-toting boat to come after us. The boat began to hum and Dylan shoved a map at Arla, but we don't need to look at it. We both knew that Tuff was one of the three islands I was tapping at just an hour before.

Tuff looked like a green dandelion. An island with a dome center, trees packed the island so that it looked like a green ball. You could easily walk across it in minutes, but it survived the lake by having a heart of solid granite. A rocky beach nestled on the west shore. Dylan's aluminum boat scraped over the pebbles. Jumping out to pull the boat onto shore, I sucked air as the cold water lapped at my ankles like sharp needles. It would take another month for the water to be warm. I tied the boat off around a rock as Arla and Dylan hopped out.

"You've been here, Arla?" Dylan asked.

"Once, years ago, we did a quick shore lunch here, but I've never explored it." She was climbing up the steep granite hills of rock. Trees were growing out of cracks and fissures in the rock. They were all stunted from the wind that rolled across the lake. How trees grew here at all was a mystery. I'm staring at them and something was nagging me.

"This isn't it," I shouted out. Dylan and Arla were almost to the top. They stopped climbing. "Remember,

Rory said that the pines were big. Unless Tuff had a fire, no one can say that the pines here are big."

Dylan started to climb over some logs, "That was eighty years ago. This island could have burned. Let's get to the top." He pointed to the top ridge. "We can get a good view from the peak and maybe we can tell where Rory was heading," I looked around. The trees looked old and there was no evidence of a fire. I was ready to argue with him when I heard a yelp and my cousin disappeared.

"Dylan!" I yelled. Arla and I rushed to where he vanished. I heard nothing. Climbing over a log, I peered into a large pit. Dylan was lying motionless at the bottom. "Help me down," I pleaded to Arla. Over the edge, I rolled my legs over, my stomach scraped against the rock. She gripped my hands to slow my fall to the bottom.

I let go and dropped the last few feet. Reaching Dylan, I felt for a pulse in his neck. A strong beat pulsed against my fingertips. A groan came out, and he flicked his eyes open. "You okay?" I asked.

Stretching his hands and his legs, he moaned again. "What did I fall into?" he barely whispered.

"A big hole," I lamely said.

His eye surveyed the hole as he sat up and murmured, "This is going to hurt in the morning."

"Nothing broken?" I hoped not, because I couldn't haul him out of this hole. Arla would have a better chance than I.

"Naw. I'm good. I think I broke through some sort of cover that had rotten. It looks like I found Rory's hiding spot." He nodded to several barrels stacked to one side.

I saw what he's looking at. This was a hiding spot for someone, but not for Rory. "He never talked about hauling barrels. Plus there was no water lapping along the side of this place." I got up and tried to pry the rim off of one of the barrels. It was rusted on so I gave it a good shake. Empty. Whatever was in it was now gone.

In the corner, a rusting metal barrel sat on a fire grate. Metal tubing sprouted from the barrel, like spaghetti. The tubing coiled and wound its way to a large kettle. "Moonshine. This place was used by someone to make moonshine probably during Prohibition," I said. Helping Dylan to stand, I started to brush his clothes off. He grimaced and rubbed the back of his thigh.

"You really okay?" Arla asked from above.

"Yeah, just landed on the wood they used to stoke the fire." He moved carefully a few steps and flexed his leg.

"Henry, I think you're right about the moonshine. It's a good place, probably overlooked by the feds. They would've had moved the corn out here by boat," Arla pointed out.

"I'm glad you're okay, Dylan, because there's no way I could get you out of here. Arla would've had to do it." I joked, but I was glad he didn't break his leg.

"He'd have to stay there and rot till he moved himself. I'm not moving his butt anywhere." Arla called out. At that point a rope came flinging from above. "Just so you don't think that I don't care. I did go and get a rope."

"Wow, thanks, Arla, Your kindness is killing me." Dylan gave a hard yank. Arla squeaked and scrambled, nearly being pulled in.

"You do that again, Thunderhead, and you can crawl out by yourself. Now wait. I'll tie this off. Then you guys can pull yourselves out." Dylan waited for Arla to show herself and then gave a big tug. It held. He climbed up the rope easily. Dang, he was strong. As soon as he went over the rim, I grabbed the rope and tried to climb up. My feet were not moving up the side as easily as Dylan's.

"Hold on," Dylan said from above. I felt a pull and Dylan easily lifted me up the side. Arla latched onto my arm and pulled me over the edge. Dylan began to coil the rope as Arla helped me up.

"Are you okay, Henry?" she asked.

"I'm the one that fell through the rotting boards," Dylan complained.

"Yeah, but you landed on your butt. You're okay. Henry dove in to save you. You're not hurt at all?" her voice was heavy with concern.

It was nice that Arla fussed over me, but I didn't want her to think I was completely helpless. "I'm fine. Really. Dylan might be hurt." I pointed as he was heading back down towards the boat. The rope was over his shoulder and he was limping.

A flash of concern crossed her face, "He's fine," she said, but she started down after him.

Dylan was untying the boat from the rock. "Let's start back. The other island is going to have to wait. Looks like bad weather's coming." I looked towards the west and a thick line of clouds were starting to roll in. The waves were starting to roll with the wind that felt icy cold against my face. "Push us off will you, Henry?" Dylan got in and lowered the motor. Arla settled down in the middle. I pushed and jumped at the same time. The boat glided out and the motor rattled to a start.

"Hang on," Dylan said. "We're going to get wet." He was turning the boat back to the cabin. The bow bounced over whitecap waves. It was a rough ride. The sky opened up, and the rain lashed at us by the time we hit the dock. The boat bucked against the dock, and I was stuffing bumpers all along the edge to prevent damage to the boat. Sheets of rain were coming down as I ran for the cabin. When I looked back to check on them, I saw Dylan limping with his arm around Arla.

Fourteen

DYLAN PEELED OFF HIS WET JEANS for his flannel sweat pants. The back of his thigh was an angry red bruise. Arla made ice packs and placed them around his leg.

"I thought you landed on your butt. You didn't break anything, did you?" Arla actually looked concern.

"No, but it's really, really sore," he whined. "Really, really hurts, Arla. I'd feel better if I had something to eat. Like a sandwich or some soup," he loudly begged. Just when Arla began to be nice to him, he behaved like a spoiled brat. I started to get up to find something to eat, but he quickly said, "Arla makes sandwiches, really good sandwiches. I would really like an Arla sandwich." He hesitated just for a moment. "If it's not too much trouble."

Arla gave him a cold stare, then a smirk appeared, "You poor baby. Of course I'll be happy to make you a sandwich. You just sit there and I'll be right back." She clomped off to the kitchen beckoning me to follow.

"Too bad, his mouth didn't get hurt," she mumbled as she opened the fridge. Uncle Mike had stocked the place with food. Turkey and cheese came out. She reached in again and pulled out a bottle of hot sauce. "This will make him feel so much better."

I'm not sure if anything could keep Dylan's mouth shut. I watched as Arla slathered hot sauce over bread and in between every slice of cheese and turkey. She squirted some mustard and mayo on top and slapped the sandwich together. Grinning, she marched back to Dylan and handed him the sandwich. She sweetly said, "This will make you feel so much better. Enjoy!"

I poured a big glass of juice and went to watch the show. I had to give Dylan credit. He must have known that she would do something. Instead he said, "I so appreciate this, thank you," and took a big bite. At first I thought when he closed his eyes, he was going to gag, but nope. He slowly chewed like he was savoring walleye and then swallowed. He gave her a quick smile and said, "This is special, only you could make a sandwich like this." Another bite went down and Arla got mad and stomped back to the kitchen. As soon as she turned her back, he motioned for the juice. The whole glass of juice was gone in one long gulp. He barely whispered, "Did she use the whole bottle on this?"

"Only half." I said as drops of sweat trickled down the side of his face.

"I can't feel my tongue anymore," he barely said. "The worst," he gagged.

"Stop eating it," I said.

"Are you kidding? I'm eating every bite and hope she feels guilty."

"She's not going to feel guilty."

"She should. The sandwich is hot enough to peel the skin off the roof of my mouth. I'm eating every bite."

"Well, then she won." My poor cousin didn't realize Arla was only going for the reaction. "She wants you to complain, so she can call you a wimp. Since you're not going to complain, she's going to see if you're dumb enough to eat the whole sandwich."

He sat the rest of the sandwich down. "Oh."

Arla marched back in with two sandwiches and handed one to me. She eyed the partially eaten sandwich on Dylan's plate, "Stop coaching him, Henry. He would've eaten the whole thing and be sick the rest of the day."

I carefully looked at my sandwich, peeling back the layers. No hot sauce dripped anywhere. I handed it to Dylan. "Let me take care of this," I murmured and took the rest of his sandwich to the kitchen. It was still raining hard. The lake was called rainy for a reason. The often daily rains were sudden, but short. This looked like an all-day drencher. The clouds hung low and heavy with rain. I made another sandwich as the rain rolled down the window.

Arla came back into the kitchen with her empty plate. Looking at the steady stream of water outside she announced, "I have to get back. Pete's almost done with his shift and this rain is here for the day. I might as well get wet now so I have time to dry out."

"Wait for Dad to give you a ride," Dylan hobbled into the kitchen. "He'll get home soon with all this rain."

"Or he'll sit at his desk, catching up with paperwork," she added. "I better take off now and get it over with."

Dylan reached for his hoodie. "I'll go with you."

"I'll go," I said quickly grabbing his hoodie. "You can barely walk, let alone ride a bike. I can do this." I gave Arla my hoodie. It fit her better than Dylan's. We'll be dry for a few seconds before the rain soaks us.

"Really, I think Dad'll be home soon. Just wait for him to give you a ride," Dylan said.

"Maybe," Arla responded. "You can have the fun harassing me tomorrow if he does and I look like a drowned rat for nothing. Henry, I can make it back okay. No use the both of us getting wet."

"It's okay. I need the exercise, so I can carry Dylan around," I said. Dylan snickered in the background. "I'll be right back," I yelled as we dashed into the rain.

The rain was still coming down in sheets. We were soaked even before we got on the bikes. By the time we were on the road, we could barely see in front of us. We looked like swamp creatures with our hoodies soaking wet, hanging to our knees. The bikes sliced through the water running across the road in wide bands. The soaked hoodie crept down over my eyes. I looked over and saw Arla's hood inching down her face. We were almost blind with wet fleece. The drum of the rain got louder. I started to laugh. The rain was warm. I wouldn't melt. So what if it was raining? I heard Arla laugh in return. Soon we were pedaling through the deepest puddles.

We were almost to the Last Stop when the truck came. Its headlights were on high blinding us in the dark of the storm. We moved to the side and prepared to be splashed from head to toe. I kept glancing up as the truck approached. I don't know what clued me in that something wasn't right. Maybe it was the revving of the truck's engine or the angle of the truck but suddenly I knew it meant to run us down.

"Watch out," I yelled. Arla rolled off into the water-swollen ditch. I leaped as the truck clipped my wheel. The impact sent me flying. I landed in the drainage ditch, knee high in water, but nothing seemed broken as I sloshed my way to Arla. She was fighting the bike, trying to push it off her. I gave the handlebars a jerk and she stood up. We climbed out of the ditch, the rain still pouring down. I checked the road. The dark pickup truck had turned around and was coming back. I wanted to think it was an accident. The truck owner must be coming back to check on us. We had just pushed the bike to the edge of the road when I heard the truck sped up again.

"He's back!" I screamed. Rushing towards her, I grabbed the soggy hoodie and yanked her back out of the road as the truck slammed into the bike. This time I concentrated on seeing the driver, but the window was too rain soaked. But I recognized the truck. The dark-gray Ford 150 that sped away was exactly like the one the Helgasons were driving the night we saw them down at the dock.

Fifteen

BY THE TIME UNCLE MIKE came to pick me up, I'd inhaled two cups of hot chocolate and at least a dozen chocolate chip cookies still warm from the oven. Gammy made us wrap ourselves up in old quilts after a hot shower. I pulled my clothes still warm from the dryer back on and they felt good. Despite two dives into the ditch neither of us had broken any bones. We only had a few bruises and a couple of small scrapes.

I wished I could read Uncle Mike better. It was a combination of relief, concern, and mad that passed over his face as I told him about the truck. I had to go over it twice and then he reconfirmed it with Arla, who didn't see who was driving the truck either, only that it was a gray Ford 150. He didn't mention the name Helgason nor did I say it, but I could see his face darken as soon as I described the truck.

The rain had stopped by the time I got into his truck. Gammy had called Uncle Mike on her marine radio. He must have been somewhere far, because it took almost an hour for him to arrive.

"Do you need to get back to work?"

"I'm good, Henry." The truck shifted into gear as he headed for the cabin. "You know Henry, the Ford 150 is a very common truck up here."

Trucks are standard up here. It's a rough country with its share of gravel roads and always lots of gear that needed to be hauled.

"Yes," I replied. He doesn't have to tell me that it could have been anyone's gray truck. I looked for the spot where our bicycles were tossed. Arla pushed hers back to the store. A tire was flat but looked repairable. My bike's handlebars stuck out of the ditch as I pointed to the spot.

"Stay here," is all Uncle Mike said as he got out of the truck twenty yards from the bike. He took a careful look at the road and saw the tire tracks edging the ditch. He pulled a camera from his pocket. Pictures from every angle were taken including my bike that was sticking out of the muck. The rain has washed a lot of the detail away, but he took about fifty shots before he stuck the camera back into his pocket. He leaned over and picked up the bike with one hand. The wheel clipped by the truck was crushed. I cursed. That bike was my only form of transportation for the summer. Looks like I was going to be walking everywhere. I heard the bike placed in the truck bed. Uncle Mike returned to the truck. He was about to shift in gear when he looked down the road and narrowed his eyes.

He reached under the dashboard and pulled out his gun. He slipped it down by his side. "Just stay in the truck and be quiet, okay?"

I barely could nod my head, because heading straight for us was the gray Ford 150.

The truck pulled up alongside and Phil Helgason, the oldest brother, rolled down his window. "I'm looking for you," he growled.

"You found me," Uncle Mike said.

"I've got business to report."

Uncle Mike looked over to me and then back at Helgason, "Okay."

"I think someone stole my truck."

If Uncle Mike was surprised, he doesn't show it, "How's that?"

"I was over visiting my mom and when I came out, my truck had been moved."

"Were the keys left in it?"

"Well, ya, I was just going to run in for a minute to let her know that Nick was in jail."

Uncle Mike grabbed his report book and started to write. "Did you see anyone take it?"

"Nope, like I said, I was in visiting my mom and telling her all about how you falsely arrested my brother. She was upset and I stayed a bit trying to calm her."

"Is anything missing from your truck?"

He took a quick glance around, "Can't tell, but I might not notice for a while."

"Anything broken?"

"Not that I can tell. I want a report about it."

Uncle Mike shifted in his seat. "I'll do that. So from what time did you stay with your mother?"

111

Helgason rubbed his whiskered face making a rasping sound, "Well, let's see. It was right after you arrested my brother until now."

"Noted and I'll write up the report. Come down to the station tomorrow and sign a statement."

"Since I have to come down that way, can I pick up my brother?" Helgason inquired.

"Not unless he suddenly has an alibi for the time of the shooting."

"He's innocent," he yelled. "He's in jail under false pretenses."

"Then he'll be released when proven he's innocent."

"You're just itching to put us away for something. This murder isn't going to be it." Helgason slammed his foot on the gas and peeled out.

"Well, that's no way to treat your tires," Uncle Mike said wearily. He looked at me and said, "How convenient that his truck was stolen. Let's get home and see what Dylan has cooked for supper."

Wait, Dylan couldn't stand. We're going to have to confess that we went out on the lake. My stomach got a funny sinking feeling. I didn't like lying to Uncle Mike. "Sounds good," was all I could think to say as we headed for the cabin.

Sixteen

"WHAT HAPPENED?" was the first thing Dylan asked as we walked into the kitchen. He was sitting at the table with a lake map rolled out over set plates and silverware. The aroma of pasta and cheese filled the room. Dylan was looking smug.

I gave him a quick review of the truck rundown. "Are you guys okay?" he asked. I reassured him we were fine, but the bike may be terminal.

"There are spare bike parts in the garage. You might be able find enough parts to get it working. It's a good project for tomorrow," Uncle Mike said as he sat down. "Smells great. Is it Mom's macaroni and cheese?"

"Yep," He started to get up, but grabbed his leg. "Hey, Henry, my leg fell asleep, can you take the casserole out of the oven?"

Clever, I thought. "No problem," I replied. I used a couple of potholders and slid a bubbly cheesy dish out of the oven. "Looks awesome."

"It does," Uncle Mike looked around the clean kitchen "The place looks good, guys. You made good use of a rainy day."

"Thanks, but notice that we're not having fish. They've moved out of the bay, Dad. When do you think it is safe to travel the lake again?" Dylan dug into the casserole and filled his plate, but kept an eye on his dad's reaction.

Silent, Uncle Mike grabbed the spoon and piled his plate high. After a moment he said, "Just a few more days. We should be getting the ID on the victim soon. I'd rest easier if I could understand the connection with our victim and suspect. You can go out a bit further, just use common sense." He chewed a cheesy spoonful when his walkie talkie went off. Pulling the communicator from his side he pushed the button and muttered, "Yes," and shoveled a quick bite in. He listened for a moment and then said, "I'll be right there."

"Phil Helgason's down at the jail. I won't be too late. Just leave the dishes. My turn to do them." He took one more bite and headed for the door.

"We'll try to leave you some." My first plateful was gone, and I was reaching for another helping. Uncle Mike stopped, quickly shoved in another mouthful. He kiddingly snarled at me and was gone.

Dylan gave a long sigh. "I thought I was going to get caught for sure. It was just luck that I didn't have to move."

"How did you cook and get everything done?"

"Sat for most of it. Mom's casserole dish is easy, a mix it up and put in the oven type dish. The rest, I just hobbled around."

"How bad is your leg?"

"Sore and stiff, but nothing's broken." He flexed his leg and stood. He started to stack plates.

"Hey, you cooked. I'll cleanup for Uncle Mike." I finished my plate and start to haul everything to the sink. Dylan took a step, wobbled and held onto the wall. "Need help?" I asked.

"Just bring the map over to the couch." He limped out of the kitchen. I heard a thud as he crashed onto the couch.

Ten minutes later we were unrolling the map. "Since the moonshine still was here," I pointed to Tuff, "that means that someone was moving moonshine in the area. I don't think Rory would even get close if he thought he was going to be seen by someone."

"Let's cross off Tuff." Dylan pointed to the island southeast of Tuff. "This is Jack's Island. We'll pick up Arla in the morning, since she seems to work afternoons and head over there."

I was thinking of Uncle Mike's words of using common sense. "Is that within your dad's boundary of a 'bit further'?"

"We'll beg forgiveness and plea stupidity if we get caught."

My hand was stretching across the map from the cabin to Jack's. "It's almost to Arla's island." That meant a good forty minute boat ride. Every warning bell was going off that this was another of Dylan's bad ideas.

"Exactly. We can fish and then head over there for shore lunch."

My gut was getting all twisted up. I always guessed wrong anyways. We haven't had fish for days. The plan sounded better by the second. "Your leg's hurt. Can I drive your boat?"

"I'm not dead, yet."

I got that cold shiver down my back.

Seventeen

THE EAGLE ALARM CLOCK woke me up. The bird was staring at me, demanding I should get up. I couldn't fall back asleep, so I made my way downstairs. Uncle Mike was sitting at the kitchen table looking more relax for the first time in days. I popped bread in the toaster and poured myself some juice. "How's it going?"

"Could be better, but okay," he poured himself another cup of coffee. I think he was still on his first pot.

"Did you find out who the guy was that got killed?'

"Nope. I got the report from the coroner yesterday and sent out inquiries yesterday. Hope to hear soon. What's up for today?"

I started to stammer. I couldn't lie to him. I finally got out, "Same stuff as always, fishing and eating." Uncle Mike gave me a funny look.

"Arla, too?"

"Yep, she keeps us in line."

Uncle Mike chuckled loud, "I bet she does. Just remember, Henry, everyone respects her in this town. We all know she single-handily is holding that store together. They barely make ends meet, for someone so young to have so much responsibility . . ." he paused. "Well, we all like her a lot. I'm glad she can get away and relax a bit." He glanced at the clock and pointed to his watch. "I've got the 6:00 a.m. shift this week. You guys get some big ones. We're being deprived of fish in this house," he said as he rinsed his cup out. He nodded goodbye and was out the door.

Did he just give permission to roam the lake? He wanted Arla to get some fun in. He wanted us to get some big ones. Neither of those goals could be achieve by sitting in the small bay. A small portion of my nagging conscious felt relieved as I went to wake up Dylan.

Dylan's leg was a marbled black and blue, "It looks bad and hurts like crazy, but I think it's getting better." He pulled down the leg of his boxers to hide it.

"Yikes, Dylan, that doesn't look better to me," I said. He ignored me. Doing a combination of hopping and hobbling, he headed for the kitchen looking for breakfast. At least his appetite had not been affected.

"Let me eat, and then I going to soak this leg in hot water so I can walk on it." He finished one bowl and started on another.

I stared at him like he's crazy. "Dylan, it looks really bad, maybe we should rest it up today."

He waved me off, "I'll be fine. I've got a feeling we're going to find Rory's hiding spot today. I'm going to soak it for a while." He struggled towards the bathroom.

"I think you're supposed to ice it the first twenty-four hours. Soaking it in hot water will make it worse," I gingerly told him. I didn't want to admit I'd learned that at a first aid camp.

Dylan gave me a sad look, "Please don't tell me you learned that in a summer camp, Henry. I'm taking a shower. Then we're heading out to pick up Arla."

He limped to the bathroom and closed the door. Dylan thought I was a complete geek, an academic nerd. So far school work had not helped me catch a bigger fish or even learn to swim. Dylan was a good student, but he was a straight "A" student in survival. I still struggled to tie my line, or catch a fish, let alone cook it over a fire. No wonder he never let me run his boat. I was like the little brother tagging behind, always expecting the big brother to bail him out. There was only one problem. I was not the little brother.

The last dish was put away. I decided to load up the boat while Dylan finished his shower. I had the fishing rods, tackle, and bait bucket for the shiners Arla would bring. Dylan came down to the dock limping, but not as bad. So much for first aid camp. He slapped me hard on the back. "We didn't get to those swimming lessons, but how about I demonstrate how to run the boat?"

"You always demonstrate how to run the boat. I sit in front for balance and you steer."

"No, really, this time you sit in the middle and sit towards me and I'll walk you through the steps. It's an old cranky Evinrude. You'll need a light hand with her."

I was waiting for the punch line. I couldn't believe he was serious. Protecting his leg, he carefully slid down by the engine and waited for me to throw the ropes in. I shoved off and sat on the middle seat.

"The first thing you need to do is make sure the prop is in the water." He pulled the latch behind the motor and lowered the prop end into the water. "Now you have to prime it. That's the rubber bulb on the line leading from the gas tank to the engine. You squeeze it to get gas to the engine, but only a couple of times. Too much and it floods the engine, and it won't start. Too little and it won't start."

I watched him squeeze the bulb four times, "Is there a big difference between a cold start and a warm start?" I asked.

"When it sits all night or even a couple of hours, do four pumps. Otherwise on a warm day or if you just cut it off, try two. Next, I have to pull the choke and place the engine in neutral." He pulled a knob in front of the engine all the way out and pushed a lever to a white line that was neutral or the idle position. "Now you pull and if it starts to run, twist the handle to give it some gas." Pulling on the starter cord the engine did nothing but a quick cough. "You try again." He pulled and the engine sputtered a few times. Dylan twisted the handle and gave the engine some gas. The engine caught and roared to a loud beat. I gave a thumbs up. Dylan swiped the lever to "run" and we left the shore behind.

I moved to the front seat to balance the load. "That's all there's to it," he shouted. Well, that was all there was if it started right away. I'd seen Dylan tinker with the motor for an hour or more to get it to run. I hoped when it was my turn I could get it to start on the first pull.

We pulled up to the dock at the Last Stop, tied the boat down and took the bait bucket into the shop. It was early, but Arla, Gammy and Pete were all working. Fishermen waited in line at the bait counter. Tanks full of shiners, rainbows, chubs, suckers, or leeches bubbled as people proclaimed they wanted a dozen or a scoop. Arla was smiling, helping customers. She poured the bait fish into plastic bags, gave them a squirt of oxygen, and twisted them closed. She gave us a quick "can't go now" look and Dylan stepped behind the counter.

Pete was handling the line for groceries and gas. He looked over his shoulder with an appreciative nod. Gammy filled out the licenses and rung up the totals. Dylan grabbed a pitcher and with a smile asked the next fisherman what he wanted.

"I think I want rainbows," he pointed to the minnows that glittered red, blue, and gold.

"Good choice," Dylan said, "that's what they're biting on." Arla chuckled behind his back. He scooped a dozen and poured them in a bag as though he had done it a thousand times. His hint on bait sent a ripple through the line and suddenly everyone was asking for rainbows.

Arla and Dylan worked side by side, filling orders and giving out tips on where to fish and how to set up lines. Pete called out from the counter asking if she needed help, but she gave a rare smile to Dylan and called back. "We're good."

Arla sent a wink towards me, and I decided to wander the store and see if I could be of help. There was a guy over at the rope section. Large spools of ropes and chains of all sizes hung from the ceiling. He was pondering the inch thick polypro.

"Can I help? Half inch and one inch comes in polypro and sisal. Polypro is best for water if you're going to use it on a boat," I said. I wanted to sound like I knew what I was talking about. "Depends on what you want to use it for."

The guy gave a slight smile. He looked familiar, like I'd seen him here before. Plaid shirt, jeans and lightweight boots for summer use. I thought I knew him, but I couldn't place him. "It's for fishing. How about thirty yards of that polypro?" I stuck the half-inch blue rope into a yard counter and started to pull. At thirty yards, I cut and heat seared the end so it won't fray. I coiled the rope for him and walked him up to Pete.

"Thanks, Henry. We got the whole crew working this morning. Where're you guys off to this early in the morning?" Pete asked.

"Fishing," I said. "We'll hook them later. They're not going anywhere."

The guy paid for the rope and inquired, "Where do you go?"

So much for him being a local. No one from around here would ever divulge where they're catching their fish. I knew better than to give away any specific spot. "Don't know yet. I let Dylan and Arla plan the fishing, but Black Bay's always good." Black Bay was the size of a small lake.

"Thanks for the hint," he said and walked out of the store.

"So what do you think he's fishing for?" I asked Pete. "He didn't buy any bait."

Pete gave the guy a long look as he climbed into a pickup and drove away. "Oh, maybe he thinks he can hook a big one with a rope instead of a hook and line. You can't tell with tourists. He might even need it for his boat to pull his friends for tubing."

"Hey, Henry, give us another half hour, and I bet it will be safe to take off." Arla walked over from the bait tanks. "Thanks for helping. I might promote you to the cash register and give Gammy a break. It's too hard for Dylan to do. He'd have to think and punch up totals at the same time," she said, loud enough for him to hear. A spray of water from the tanks splattered her in the back. Arla gave a loud shriek.

"Careful," Dylan said, "or I'll tell everyone that earthworms are what the fish are biting on."

"No problem, I've got earthworms and leeches in the fridge. If they want them, I'll sell them," she chanted. "I even have frozen walleye fillets to bring home for those who can't catch 'em."

"How's groceries and gas selling, Pete?" she asked.

"Arla if you were here instead of me, we would sell twice as much, but we aren't doing too bad. Steady, especially with boat gas and fish fry mix. There's a lot of wishful thinking out there."

"You're so sweet, Pete," Arla cooed and I heard Dylan calling for her. She sighed, "Dylan must have forgotten how to tell the difference between shiners and chubs. Good job, Pete."

Gammy was still busy ringing up customers, so I headed over to help her out. I bagged goods, got bags of bait and carried out bags of ice. An hour went by before the business slowed, but I liked the work. You don't see grumpy people going fishing. Everyone was looking forward to a day out on the lake. They came from all over to fish. I talked to people from Virginia to Arizona. They were all looking to hook the big one. Everyone wanted to know where to fish and how to get them on their line. I could see why Gammy loved the store.

Arla came over and claimed that the rush was over. "So what should we bring . . . shiners or chubs?"

"Let's try rainbows," I said and saw Dylan grabbing a pitcher.

He looked into the tanks. "She's running low on rainbows. Shiners it is." A dozen went into our bait bucket.

"I'll be back in time to relieve Pete." Arla told Gammy.

"Go and get some fish this time. I'll be fine here till you get back." She took out some order forms and started looking through them. "It'll be quiet until people get their bait for evening fishing."

Dylan was still limping, so I made him and Arla get in the boat first. I shoved off, the wind was picking up and the waves were choppy. "We'll scout out Jack's Island first," he yelled. "We can fish off your island point after." Arla nodded. I held tight to the sides of the boat as Dylan sped up and the boat attacked the waves.

A half hour later of hard bouncing across the waves, we landed on the shore of Jack's Island. No one lived here.

The beach was hard rock. We moored the boat in shallow water to prevent it from getting beat up against the rocks and waded to shore. We dragged the anchor along the bottom until it lodged in rocks. The wind picked at the waves making the boat rock. We tied off the boat in two directions. This island was primarily granite, but pockets of dirt supported trees and some bushes. At least twice as large as Tuff, we decided to split up to search the island. We gave Dylan the deer path that wound around the island. Arla got to climb the top. I scrambled over the rocks at the shoreline to search for any type of cave.

We stuck together within calling distance as we circled the island clockwise. I didn't want to push Dylan's leg too hard. Arla was keeping an eye on him. It took us a full hour, but we found nothing. Crawling over rocks along the shore, I searched every crack and crevice for the missing cave. Arla and Dylan had no luck finding anything. We headed for the small inlet where the boat was moored when we realized that we're in trouble. The boat was still there, bobbing in the water with waves much higher than just an hour ago. It was the other boat moored right beside ours. Arla gasped. Phil and Nick Helgason were waiting for us.

Eighteen

EY PHIL, DOESN'T THAT TALL ONE belong to our friend, Officer Mike?" Stretched out, he had hooked his boots over the edge of Dylan's boat. The Helgason brothers were mirrors of each other, both had long thin blonde hair three days past due for a wash. Each had on hats sporting the local small mouth bass tournament.

Phil stopped peering into our boat and looked up. "Sure is. I saw him and the little one at the dock the night Officer Mike was harassing us. They were hiding in the truck."

He picked up a fishing rod and then dropped it. "You'd think the son of a Border Patrol man would have better stuff than this. This stuff is nothing but crap. Tell that daddy of yours to get you some good fishing gear."

Dylan and I stepped into the water, "Get away from our boat!" Dylan growled.

Quickly, my arm shot out stopping him from rushing them. "What do you guys want?" I tried to ask calmly.

"Well, see. We were thinking about going fishing, but forgot all our stuff. We were going to ask nicely if you would let us use your equipment." Nick started to laugh, "but your stuff's crap."

"Then you best go," I said. I grabbed and squeezed Dylan's arm so hard my hand started to go numb. Dylan trembled with rage. Arla stepped into the water besides us.

Phil squinted at her. "Arla, what're you doing here with these two?" He looked at the island behind them. "Wait till I tell your Gammy you're out exploring with these two."

"You go ahead and do that. You wouldn't be telling her anything new, and she'd know you two are causing trouble." Arla took another step towards them. I reached out to hold her back.

"Wow, she's got some spunk, Nick. Not very friendly of her, is she?"

"Nope, not at all. We just stopped to have a friendly visit, and I think my feelings are hurt, Phil. I don't think they like us," Nick sniggered.

Dylan was ready to lunge for them when Nick pushed away from Dylan's boat. "I guess we wore out our welcome, Phil. Make sure you tell your daddy we said, 'hi' and tell him to leave us alone. We'll be checking up on you guys." Phil started his motor and they jetted off leaving our boat bouncing in the wake.

"What jerks," Arla stared as the boat disappeared.

"Dad's going to be pissed off about this. That's a threat he gave us."

"Guys, we have another problem. The boat!" I yelled, the Helgason's parting gift was cutting our anchor and mooring ropes.

In the rough waves, the boat was fast being washed away from the island. Dylan and Arla immediately dove in. Helplessly I watched them swim out and snag the boat by the dangling ropes. Dylan helped lift Arla into the boat. She balanced the far side as Dylan rolled in. Feeling completely useless, I use my foot to locate the anchor. Chest deep in water, I took in a deep breath and ducked. My fingers took hold of anchor edge. I hauled it up. Two feet of rope was still attached. The Helgasons were jerks.

Dylan found the oar and began to paddle towards me. When he was close enough, Arla threw the cut rope. Stretching, I snagged the end and pulled to get the boat closer. The boat was bobbing in the rough water. I strained and edged the anchor up the side of the boat. Arla helped pull it in. A big wave soaked me, and I lunged for the side. The boat was pulling me fast into deeper water. My feet no longer touched the bottom. I clung to the side. I had left my life jacket in the boat and panic was twisting in my chest. Somehow, I managed to hook my leg on the side and rolled over the edge. Dripping wet and panting, Dylan lowered the engine prop as the waves bounced us around.

"Are we good? Anything missing?" I asked between breaths. I clamped my jaw to keep from chattering. For one moment I thought we were good. All three of us looked around and realized what they took.

Dylan cursed, "The life jackets."

My heart skipped a beat. I knew I had left mine in the boat. It was gone. We were so close to shore, the water was only knee deep. I had taken it off. The wind blew harder and whitecaps started to form on the wave tips.

Dylan looked at the incoming bank of dark clouds from the west. "We have to get off the lake," he stated. "Storm's coming in. We can't be out on the lake without life jackets. We'll swing behind Arla's island to get out of the wind and then try to get to shore from there. If it gets bad, we'll land at the island and wait the storm out."

Dylan pulled on the starter rope and the engine sputtered, and then died. He leaned down and tweaked the gas mixture. The wind and waves were pushing us fast into the rocks. I took the oar and shoved us away from the boulders. Again he pulled and the engine coughed and roared to life. Dylan tweaked the gas mixture again and the engine banged louder. The boat plunged through the water. I immediately got drenched by a wave that slammed across the bow.

The wall of dark clouds rolled over us and the rain came. Lightening crackled, the raindrops stung us. The fourteen-foot boat couldn't reach from wave crest to wave crest so the boat slammed down into each trough. It was like riding a bucking bronco. I looked back. Water was streaming down Arla's face. Both hands gripped the sides of the boat. Her face pinched with worry, she still sent me a smile. I cursed the Helgason brothers.

Her island was straight ahead. Dylan swung around the northeast point to gain some shelter from the wind. Immediately, the boat was not bucking so hard. The rain was still punishing, but I relaxed my death hold from the sides of the boat. Dylan and Arla were both smiling a bit.

Arla shouted, "We'll run the entire length of my is-land out of the wind. We can make it back to shore from there. The bay can protect us from the wind. We'll go around the point at Jackfish Bay and then to the Last Stop." The storm wasn't letting up but it wasn't getting worse.

We rarely explored this part of Arla's island. Steep rock cliffs had no friendly inlets, no sand beaches anywhere. We skirted dangerous rocks that lay a hundred yards from the cliffs. Dylan tried to give a wide berth to any that might be hidden just beneath the water. The boat managed the waves and my racing heart slowed. The waves were still rough, but the downpour had softened to a steady rain. I turned to shout at Dylan that it looked like we're going to make it, when I heard the faint crack of a rifle over the howling storm.

Arla's eyes told me that something bad had hap-pened. Her eyes were wide and blue, and again they re-minded me of early morning. She's stared at my hand where I gripped the side of the boat with those beautiful cornflower-blue eyes. I then realized that Dylan was shout-ing at me to get down. I couldn't. I seemed to be frozen, not with pain, but paralyzed with the knowledge that some-thing bad was coming, and I couldn't do anything about it. I looked down and saw a bullet hole right below my hand. I flexed my fingers, and they worked, so I gave a slight smile at Arla and dragged her down with me to the floor. Dylan powered the boat through a maze of rocks towards the shore.

I popped my head up to find the shooter. "They're in a boat behind us," I shouted.

"The Helgasons?" Dylan shouted back.

"No, it's the white boat."

"Keep low. I'm going to try to run the boat up on the rocks. Then we should try to hide on shore. Henry, are you okay?"

"I'm good, but the boat's taking water," I yelled out. Three inches of water sloshed in the bottom of the boat. My heart was racing. Dylan turned his motor to full speed. We were in the rocks with waves crashing around us. Rain continued to fall, adding to the water in the boat. It lapped over my ankles. I ripped my t-shirt sleeve off and tried to plug the hole, but the boat was bucking too hard.

Dylan aimed for a rocky shelf that jutted from the cliff. We almost made it.

We heard another shot and more water started to pour into the boat. It had pierced the hull at the water line. Arla screamed, and Dylan pulled hard on the tiller to give the shooter a harder shot, but a wave caught us and catapulted the boat onto the rocks. Hurled into the water, I watched Dylan be tossed against the rocks and rolled lifeless below the water. Arla disappeared beneath the waves as I felt the cold of Rainy Lake pull me down.

In June, the water in Rainy Lake stole my breath away, and I can't swim. Somehow the waves pushed me up, and I snatched a breath of air. Dylan was still gone under the waves. Arla broke the surface gasping for breath. Panic tightened every muscle in my body. I took a deep breath in and sank beneath the cold waters. Somehow my arms and legs moved, coordinated and smooth. I found Dylan beneath the churning waves. Heavy and boneless, I reached for his unconscious body, found his shirt and pulled hard. Above me was the diffuse light of the surface. Uncle Mike wasn't there to save me. I kicked hard and brought both of us up. I broke the surface, and sucked air so deeply that my lung's ached. Arla was struggling to tread water, but she helped to brace Dylan's head up. I kicked for shore.

Somehow I got there. Somehow all those lessons that Dylan tried to teach me came together. Somehow, Arla and I got Dylan to the shore and draped him over a large rock. I staggered to stand upright. My body shook, and my arms ached. I leaned over to examine my cousin's head. He had a large gash high on his forehead. It was bleeding. Arla was looking for something to staunch the flow. My fingers searched his neck hoping for a pulse. I felt the steady throb of his heart. "Wake up, Dylan!" I said and shook him gently.

He groaned and lifted one eye open. "Where am I?"

I watched the blood drip off his forehead and onto the large rock beneath him, flowing into the cracks, seeping deep into the red crevices. "Blood Rock," I said.

Nineteen

DYLAN OPENED THE OTHER EYE and looked down at the large boulder beneath him.

I scanned the lake. The white boat had disappeared. "There's no sign of them anywhere."

"Good," Arla said and she too, quickly scanned the lake. She knelt alongside the big rock. "You okay?" Arla asked Dylan. He nodded, and she ran her hand over the surface and tried to rub away some of the red that was in the cracks. She didn't wait for him to reply. She examined her fingers, "For sure it's paint."

"Hey, I'm bleeding here." Dylan reached to probe his wound. Arla stopped his hand in mid-action.

"Don't get it dirty. It's going to leave a scar and you don't want to make it worse." She reached over and ripped off the bottom part of his shirt. "I'm sure this isn't clean but it'll prevent that nasty wound from getting dirtier." She wrapped it around his head and gave it a good tug to secure it in place.

"Arla," he shouted, "the head. I feel like you're ripping it off my neck."

"What a baby. Henry nearly got shot and you don't hear him complaining."

I left them arguing. The storm was still raging, but we were protected. Looking up I saw why. A large rock overhang kept the rain off. At first, it appeared as a solid rock wall, but it was an illusion. I found a seam, a crack that followed the cliff upwards. There was an opening that we'd have to walk around the rock wall to find. Looking straight on, the opening disappeared. Stepping behind it, I looked back out and shouted, "Over here. I found Rory's hideout." That shut them up. Dylan staggered a bit when he stood up, but Arla offered her shoulder for support as they followed me into the cave.

Tree trunk logs braced the entrance, forming a wood lined hall. There high on a cross beam I ran my fingers over the letters of R.M and O.C.J. and the date of July 6, 1931, carved deep into the wood. It felt real. Rory and O.C. had been here and made their mark. Shifting my eyes to the inside, the cool, damp air penetrated my clothes. I shivered and stepped into the interior of the cave. Insulated by the storm, I heard water. Dim light and dripping water filtered down from small holes in the ceiling.

The cavern was huge. We stood in a space that was as large as a classroom. The ceiling spanned the height of the cliff and had to be forty feet high. The floor was hard granite rock and splattered with water from the ceiling. Off to one side on a pallet of logs was a stack of boxes. Arla reached to open the flaps of fragile cardboard and inside were bottles of Canadian whiskey. Pulling a bottle out, she tipped the bottle and clear amber liquor sloshed against the sides. "He didn't sell it."

I opened another case. It was full of the bottles. There were fifteen cases all full of Canadian whiskey from 1931. "Looks like he didn't get to sell any of it."

"So what happened on Hell's Point that night?" Arla replaced the bottle and dusted her hands off.

I heard a sharp gasp from Dylan. A bottle of eighty-year-old Canadian whiskey shattered on the floor. Fumes from the strong liquor assaulted my nose. Dylan gasped for breath, backing away from the stash of bottles as fast as he could.

"What's wrong?" I asked. He was the color of chalk. I was afraid he had suffered a delayed reaction from banging his head.

"What's wrong?" I said louder. Dylan shakily pointed.

Finally he said, "There. Behind the cases. There," he stammered.

Arla and I stepped slowly to the far edge of the stack of whiskey cases. She turned away and stumbled back to Dylan. I stared at the two skeletons that lay side by side behind the whiskey. They were chained together, and I had no doubt that I was looking at Rory and O.C.

Fragments of clothes clung to parts of the skeletons. They had been lying there for a very long time. Dylan came up behind me, "Whoever Rory was to meet that night was not the good guys. Do you think they were left here to starve?"

I pointed to the hole above the eye sockets of their skulls. The hole was small but it had ended their lives. "I think a bullet killed them."

"Who killed them?" Arla pondered. "Remember that Rory thought he was being watched when he went exploring the island. It could've been Al Capone's people or Baby Face Nelson or any of the other gangsters. It could've been some other bootlegger trying to cut into his business. We'll probably never know."

"He must had gotten there early and stashed the journal in the cabin and then met up with the killers, but who put the newspaper in the wall?" I heard the rain still dripping down and wondered how we're going to get out of here. Dylan's boat was smashed up on the rocks. Plus it had that problem of bullet holes.

"Hey. I think we should start thinking how to get out of here. Dylan, I don't think your boat's an option. Arla, this is your island, do you have any emergency supplies stashed somewhere?"

"You won't need any," said a voice along with the click of a gun being cocked.

Twenty

FOR A MOMENT, I THOUGHT we were going to be saved. "Pete," Arla brightly said. All I saw was a gun pointing at us, but her smile melted into a frown. "Pete, what're you doing?"

"Trying to kill you," he replied flatly.

"Why?" she looked confused. "We have nothing. The store's just hanging on." Fear passed across her face. She quickly asked, "Gammy, have you hurt her?"

"The old lady's fine. Of course, she might die from the heartbreak of losing you. But I'll hang around. When she dies, I'll take over."

"You're doing this for the store?" Arla said, disbelieving.

"Heck, no. I want this," he swung his gun around to the inside of the cave.

The wave of the firearm was like a wand. The rain had stopped. The sun came out and shot beams of light into the cave. It was like magic. The light struck the walls. The pretty pink and gray granite that Rory wrote about began to sparkle like diamonds. However, it wasn't diamonds, it was quartz laced with veins of pure gold. The whole cave glowed. We all gasped.

"It's the 'River of Gold,'" I whispered.

"Yeah, I'm going to be rich," Pete bragged. "There's probably millions of dollars here. We've been searching the lake since the ice went out. I never would have found it if not for that journal."

"How did you get hold of the journal?" I asked.

"Arla left it beneath the counter. It was a slow day, so I read it. I knew it was one of the islands around Little American or Bushyhead. I had my cousins helping me search. I just knew that vein of gold ran right through the lake."

"He was at the store the other day," I said. "Your cousin bought the rope."

"He's stupid. I told him to wait till I was there by myself, but he couldn't wait."

I remembered where I had seen him before. "He was on Little American Island, dressed like a ranger. We saw him in the mine."

"You saw him?" he said angrily, "Billy, get in here," he yelled out.

Billy walked through the entrance with the thirty feet of rope with him. "I told you," he sputtered. "I saw the boat there. I just didn't see anyone. I thought they were out exploring the island."

"It was you, who killed that guy on Bushyhead," Dylan suddenly said. "Who did you kill?"

"That was an accident," Pete quickly said.

"That was no accident," Billy screamed. "You killed my brother."

"Your brother, my cousin, was greedy, Billy. He thought because he found this cave he should get a larger cut. I told him we were going to split it. He threatened me. He was going tell Arla and try to negotiate a deal with her."

"I would've never made a deal," Arla stated.

"I tried to tell him that, but he wouldn't listen to me. So my gun accidently went off."

"Like it accidently shot at us at the beach?" I questioned.

"I know I'm a pretty good shot, but shooting from a rocking boat is impossible. I missed you, Arla, completely. If you'd died then or when I tried to run you over, your friends wouldn't be dying with you now. I would've never been caught. I could snatch this island up for a song."

"You stole Helgason's truck," I started, but Billy interrupted.

"You killed my brother, you heartless rat. He was your kin." Billy swung the coil of rope like a baseball bat. The thick bundle of rope smashed Pete on the side of the head knocking him down. A shot rang out in the cave. Billy crumpled. Blood pooled across the rock floor.

Pete was already swinging the gun towards us, threatening us to keep back. He looked at Billy and sighed. "This is going to have to get cleaned up. You guys, get over here. Drag the body out. Just throw it into the lake. The current will carry him out. They'll never find the cave."

He motioned with his gun for us to move the body. "Hurry up. Move him." Dylan and I didn't move. "Do it or I shoot her." He waved his gun at Arla.

We both started for Billy. But then we heard a strong voice, "U.S. Border Patrol. Surrender your weapon. Pete Harper, you're under arrest for the murder of your cousin, James Harper." Uncle Mike stepped into the cave, his gun in his hand.

Pete immediately jerked the gun towards Arla. "Stand back or she dies," he screamed. Sweat popped out on his face, his eyes nervously darted between Uncle Mike and us. His gun hand was shaking. I knew he was going to do something stupid.

"I mean it. I'll kill her," he screamed again.

Uncle Mike calmly took another step forward, "Lay your weapon down, Pete. I've got men stationed outside. You can't escape."

My eyes were watching Pete's trigger hand. His finger on the trigger twitched. He focused on Arla. He was going to pull the trigger. I never guess right, but I still leaped.

Twenty-One

I DON'T CONSIDERED MYSELF A HERO. I had no idea why I did what I did, but I knew Pete was going to shoot. I dove, pushing Arla to the ground. Lucky for me, I finally guessed right. Plus, Uncle Mike shot at the same time. I felt Pete's bullet go through my shirt across my shoulder. He missed Arla.

However, Uncle Mike didn't miss him. Pete was moaning on the ground complaining of the pain. Uncle Mike had gotten him in his arm and forced him to miss his mark. The cave filled with officers. Uncle Mike was cuffing Pete. Billy was alive but seriously wounded, so Uncle Mike commanded a boat to take Pete and Billy to the hospital. Uncle Mike came over and crushed us in a hug. I gave a small groan and suddenly everyone noticed that I'd gotten shot.

"Henry, you okay?" Dylan asked.

Arla pulled back the fabric from what's left of my tee shirt. "It nicked you. You're either the luckiest guy in the world or the unluckiest, because you know me." She ripped the rest of my tee shirt off and started to bind up the shoulder.

Uncle Mike was looking us all over. Dylan had drying blood all over his face and down his shirt. My shoulder was bandaged and Arla looks bruised and exhausted, "Tough day, guys. Henry, you hanging in there, okay?"

"I'm fine," I stated. I only felt a slight burn.

"You're not shocky or anything. Feel cold or shaky?"

"Not yet," I tried to sound confident. "Uncle Mike, I'm really glad to see you."

"Me, too. Henry," Uncle Mike gave me a gentle bear hug and gave us another good look over, "Let's get out of here. You all look a bit worse for wear. Looks like a trip to the hospital for some stitches."

Arla shook her head, "I have to get back to check on Gammy. I'm afraid he hurt her."

"She's fine. I just saw her. She told us you were here."

"How did she know?" Arla asked.

"She watched you take off in this general direction and you guys always come here," Uncle Mike admitted.

"You know that?" Dylan exclaimed.

"I don't blame you. It's a beautiful island. If it was mine, I'd be here all the time. "

"Did you know about this cave?" I asked. I got that feeling again that we could have saved ourselves a lot of trouble if Uncle Mike had known about the journal.

"No idea that it was here. I think it was our eagle screaming over this site. Otherwise I'm not sure that I would have found it. Once I got closer I saw the boat on the rocks."

"Did you know that Pete was the bad guy?" I inquired.

"We got the report this morning and found out the murder victim was his cousin. We pretty quickly pieced the puzzle together. The cave is a surprise. I thought I knew the lake pretty well, but this is well hidden."

"Dad, we have two skeletons over here," Dylan stated while pointing to the whiskey stash. "They're two boys from the 1930s. We think they are Rory McDougal and O.C. Jarvason."

Uncle Mike walked over to look at the remains. "How do you know their names?"

"We found a journal up in the rafters in the cabin," I said. "Rory talks about his hiding spot for his bootleg whiskey. We thought it would be fun to find it." Fun that nearly got us killed. I was already trying to figure out a way to tell my folks that I got shot and still let me stay up here for the summer.

"I'll need to take a look at the journal. You found it up in our attic?"

"We stumbled upon it. It's at my place," Arla said.

"I'm going to let one of the officer's get you home, Arla. Dylan and Henry need stitches. We'll stop over after the hospital to collect the book." Another strong beam of sunlight shot through and again the cave walls glittered and sparkled. "Very pretty. Arla, this cave is beautiful, usually you don't get this much quartz in with the granite."

Dylan ran his hand over the wall. "The gold, Dad. How much do you think it is worth?"

Uncle Mike gave a big grin and chuckled. "It's fool's gold, Dylan. I'm afraid that it's not worth much except that it's beautiful." Arla sighed in disappointment.

My heart fluttered a bit. I thought we had found millions. "We thought it was the 'River of Gold,' the gold mine of the Indian legend," I blurted out.

"Afraid not. That legend has been around forever. I looked for it when I was a kid. If it's true or not is still to be proven. For now though we need to get you guys stitched up."

Dylan and I boarded one of the Border Patrol boats and headed for the nearby hospital. Arla was sent home on a smaller boat that now skimmed a quieter lake after the storm. I buckled up the life jacket that was handed to me. I saw what was left of the Dylan's boat. One half was bobbing in the water, the other half was grating against rocks. Dylan had a sick look on his face.

Uncle Mike sat down besides us. "Good job, guys. Dylan, your boat will survive. You must've put the foam in under the seats I gave you."

"Yeah, I did that before Henry got here. In case we flipped the boat, I knew it'd float and he'd have something to hang on to," he said. "Waste of time, Henry can swim like a fish. He saved my life." He started to pound me on my sore shoulder, but then pulled back. "I'll skip the arm punch, but thanks for saving me."

"We're good," I said. "I've no idea how I swam. I just saw you log rolling off the rocks and swam for you. I'm sure it was pretty ugly." I was going to have to bribe Arla not to tease me about my swimming technique. I had a feeling I must have looked like a flopping fish.

"I think the boat's still salvageable." Uncle Mike stated, "I'll have it towed over to our place. It'll need work, but it'll give you something to do while you're both grounded." We both groaned. "For a week. Henry the real punishment will be you trying to explain what happened to your parents and how you got shot. And I want no lying by omission. Full disclosure because I'll follow up."

I groaned again. Impossible. My parents would go nuts. My shoulder even stopped burning for a while as I tried to think of a way to stay up at the cabin the rest of the summer.

At the hospital, it felt like they used a wire brush to clean out the gunshot wound. It was really just a scratch, even though they insisted in putting in a few stitches. I practiced saying "only a few stitches" several times in my head to make it sound minor. Dylan got eight in his head, but they were tiny.

I walked out of the ER, and Uncle Mike handed me his cell phone. My parents were silent on the other end. The fact that both of them were on the phone and they were quiet meant there wasn't a chance to make this sound positive. So I spilled everything, from start to finish. By the time I was done begging to let me stay up here for the rest of the summer, we were at Arla's. I heard nothing on the phone after my pleading. Finally my dad shocked me and said, "Okay." I almost cried in relief. After a moment of gratitude, I handed the phone back to Uncle Mike.

"Yeah, Dylan, I think he confessed all." He listened then said, "That was not entirely my fault, and it happened over thirty years ago. We were just kids. Holding onto grudges that long is bad for you, besides that scar hardly shows anymore." He listened again, "Okay, Dylan," he said loudly. "I promise I'll watch him and, yes, I know he's your only son." He hung up and gave us a smile. "You're good, but you're still grounded for a week."

It would take that long before they could take out our stitches, so I just nodded. Arla and Gammy were sitting behind the counter. The store was quiet, and Gammy was looking at the journal, running her hands over the pages.

"Gammy was able to fill in some details for us," Arla started. "I'd never heard this and it explains a lot."

Gammy picked up the journal and held it to her heart. "You filled in a lot of missing holes in my life today. I thought I'd never be able to find the answers. This explains so much. Sit down and I'll try to explain."

Arla had already filled some bowls with vanilla ice cream. We all sat down and Gammy began.

"I was born December of 1930 as a Jarvason. My brother was O.C. His real name was Otis Charles. I didn't know he hated that name. In fact, I don't have any memories of him or my father. Everything was lost in the fire. The journal was correct that my mother died when I was born. I was still a baby when I was brought to Rory's mom. After the boys disappeared, she adopted me, and I can't imagine how hard it must've been to take care of three little girls. She remarried later that year, a man involved in the timber trade and for a short time we lived in that cabin out on Hell's Point."

"I believe it must've been her who put the paper in the wall, maybe to lock away a part of her loss. Maybe she left it as a clue, hoping that someone someday would find out what happened to Rory and O.C. I know she didn't know about this journal. She talked about the boys often and the journal would've been mentioned. My stepfather did die when a mule kicked him and both my sisters died young in a car accident. When my adopted mom passed on, I was given the island. It had been in Rory's family for a while and now's a part of ours. I never knew about the cave, but I want to bury my brothers in the family plot."

She looked at Uncle Mike and he nodded, "Of course, I'll make sure their remains are released to you."

"I have one picture of them, taken that spring the summer they disappeared." She handed us a picture frame with a black-and-white photo of two boys on Blood Rock, their arms across each other's shoulders, just good friends enjoying the lake on a sunny day. Rory was blond and good looking while O.C. was dark-haired with bright eyes that I swore if the photo was in color would be cornflower blue. I studied the picture and tried to imagine them hanging out together. I knew how it felt to have a really good friend, even grounded for a week.

"We'll probably never find out who killed them," Dylan said.

"I'm not sure it matters. They were doing illegal bootlegging and were bound to get caught," Gammy acknowledged.

"As for the whiskey in the cave, I did some calling around while the guys were getting stitched up, and I think the local historical society would give you a fair price for it. It has historical value. They'd like it for their collection." Uncle Mike claimed. "They might even have a freezer they'd trade for."

Arla nearly cheered, "I'd pay someone to get rid of that old clunker."

I was just glad that ice cream would be at the store. Uncle Mike borrowed the journal, and we packed ourselves into the truck. My shoulder was starting to ache. Dylan claimed his headache was bad enough to make his eyes cross. The cabin never looked better. Dylan's boat had been brought up on shore and was lying down by the boathouse. Uncle Mike told us to go relax and he'd fix supper.

We both crashed on the couch too numb to move. "The Helgasons," I mumbled. I had completely forgotten about their threat. They took our life jackets. Uncle Mike was going to be mad.

"Let's give that one a rest till at least tomorrow," Dylan suggested. "We should give it a few days until this murder case is tied up. Trust me, he'll get furious. He may ban us from being out on the lake until he talks to them."

"Good idea," I said, but I got a feeling it wasn't a good idea. I was just too exhausted to protest.

"The gold's still out there, Henry. We've the rest of the summer to find it." Dylan gave me a look that meant the boat would be up and running by the end of the week.

I swore my stomach started to cramp.

Acknowledgments

Rainy Lake did have a gold rush in 1893, with gold mining on Little American, Big American, Lyle Mine, and Soldier's Mine. The area was flooded with new immigrants hoping to make it rich. By 1894, the gold rush town of Rainy Lake City was established on the Kabetogama Peninsula. These early pioneers built shops, banks, schools, a brick factory, and seventeen saloons. The gold was never plentiful. By 1901, operations had ceased and dreams had died. Gold revenues amounted to only $5,000 and Rainy Lake City disappeared. Now the mines are a part of the history preserved by the Voyageurs National Park.

The gold found at the original mine at Little American Island was embedded in the quartz that was part of the Rainy Lake-Seine River fault. Like other earthquake faults, the Rainy Lake-Seine River fault is long. It stretches 174 miles through the middle of Rainy Lake. The fault line has long been dormant, but some think that gold might still be found. A big thank you to the National Park Service for providing information and preserving our historical sites.

So many people have helped me with this book. Their advice and feedback made this book what it is today. I want to give thanks to my husband, Jeffrey; my sons, Brian and Alex; and my parents, Lawrence and Ann. Thank you to the editors at North Star Press for their insight and making my dream a reality. My thanks to Kerry Temple for teaching me to love revisions. The annual summer SCBWI meeting gave me the lucky draw to be critiqued by an incredible author, Kathleen Duey. Thank you! It was a turning point for me and your advice was right on. To my fearless writer's group of Joan, Cheryl, Marcy and Tina, who gave me feedback, I couldn't have done it without you. Thank you, Lou, for your expertise and patience; you're a great teacher and friend. To my first readers and tireless listeners, Kathie, Susie, Greg, Sarah, Autumn, Ariel, Forrest, Erica, Ray, Jennifer, Chuck, Madelyn, and William, thank you for asking me that all-important line: "but then what happened?" I'll be forever grateful.